MISTLETOE MISHAPS

TRACY BROEMMER

Mistletoe Mishaps

by

Tracy Broemmer

Contemporary Romance Novella

Published by Tracy Broemmer

Edited by Lexie Broemmer

Cover Graphics: Deposit Photos

Cover Design by: Redbird Designs

Copyright © 2020

ISBN#: 978-1-951637-15-6

A big thank you to Ellie Mack, who put together the anthology that made me decide to write Mistletoe Mishaps.
Thank you, Kate Carley, for being an awesome critique partner and even more for being my bestie in the book world.

For everyone who loves to decorate for Christmas, the bigger, the better! I have very fond memories of decorating the whole house with my mom when I was a kid.
And since my husband and I have been married—27 years now! —we have driven around every Christmas Eve after Midnight Mass to look at lights. The 2018 Christmas Eve midnight ride inspired this story.

ONE

NIC COLLIER HUNG HER HEAD AND HUFFED OUT ANOTHER irritated sigh. She *hated* Christmas lights, and right about now, she hated her house and the gutter and the light clips and the ladder she stood on and the neighbor who had called a greeting to her—oh yeah, he'd sounded a little amused and a lot smug—and she swallowed down a prickly, niggling little jolt of hatred for Hailey Gerritsen. The very same Hailey Gerritsen that the rest of the world loved.

Okay, maybe not the *whole* world, but pretty much everyone in Nic's world, and maybe hatred was a bit strong, but also pretty damned close at the moment. After all, it was Hailey's fault that she was all but hanging from her gutter, stringing up the damned icicle lights that were at least a few years out of style.

"Nic?"

Damn. And let's not forget the part about Scott Woodrow standing at the foot of her ladder. Holding it steady for her. She almost jumped, because that last wave of frustration with Hailey had trumped everything else, and she had forgotten that Scott was here. To help her.

She rolled her eyes and groaned quietly as she lifted her chin.

"Hmm?" She didn't trust herself to speak.

"You okay up there?"

Why was he here? Well, yeah, he was helping her put up her Christmas stuff. Nic got that much. Hailey had probably sent him over, but Nic had told him she was fine. She didn't need help. He could go. He hadn't, though. He hadn't left, and he was helping, and he'd offered at least seven times now to do this part. To climb the ladder and hang the lights.

"Yep."

"You sure you don't want me—?"

Eight.

She dropped her head back to hang between her shoulder blades. Her hands hurt from the cold.

"I'm fine, Scott," she mumbled.

"Can I make a suggestion?"

Nic flexed her fingers as she turned slowly on the ladder and shot him a look that said *I'm all ears.* But she bit her tongue when she met his cobalt blue gaze. How could one guy be that cute *and* nice? Scott Woodrow was dreamy; she'd noticed that a year ago when he'd been new on the crew and Hailey had introduced him to Nic and the rest of the gang. He was tall and a little lanky, but not in a bad way. His long legs weren't awkward, so much as lean and sexy—not that Nic looked. Much. He had wide shoulders and a tapered waist, and Nic had most definitely noticed his butt. What female on the planet wouldn't notice Scott Woodrow's butt?

Best of all? He was nice. No false advertising in his friendly smile. He was mild-mannered, handled himself professionally, sure, but he was fun, too. Always had time to help anyone out. Which, Nic supposed, was why he had shown up here earlier.

She nodded slowly. As a news producer, Nic was used to doling out orders and taking charge. Most of the crew had been together for five years, and Nic rarely had to flex her bossy muscles. But she could and did now and then.

Not with Scott, though. Nope.

"Sure." She arched her eyebrows and waited for him to suggest she get down and let him finish the lights for her. She wouldn't. She'd thank him and go back to wondering why the damn lights weren't working, and he'd go back to watching her. Either until they were finished or until one of them froze to death.

Doubtful. It was just cold enough to be miserable, but certainly not freezing.

"C'mere." He reached for her hand.

Well, *this was new*. She squeezed her hand into a fist again and then backed down the ladder to the first rung, so she was standing almost eye to eye with him.

"What if…" He took her hand, even though she'd just moved down to look at him. "We…scrapped these lights. And went to get new ones."

They'd worked together for a year. They were work friends. Period. She blinked at her fingers, encircled in his big warm hand. Warm? How was his hand warm?

"New ones?" She cleared her throat and looked up to find those blue eyes searching her face intently. He nodded, but rather than speak, he stepped toward her into the bushes where she'd had to wedge the ladder. His eyes never left her face, so Nic was careful not to look away, though she wondered what he was doing. Why was he getting so close?

"New lights," he repeated. When he squeezed her fingers, she nodded. New lights. Of course. Why hadn't she thought of that? But he didn't step back, didn't look away. Instead, he leaned further into her. Nic caught her breath when she felt him touch her cheek with his free hand. He stroked his thumb over her lower lip and dropped his gaze there when she gasped in surprise again.

He was—what the—oh!—he was going to kiss her. Yep. He had that look, that intense look that guys in the movies get just before they kiss the girl. Before Nic could process that, before she could react, Scott brushed his lips —warm and soft—over hers.

Okay, proof that she wasn't frozen yet, because her heart fluttered up her chest and throat, and a wave of warmth unfurled through her belly and fingertips. Still in his hand, her fingertips throbbed, and Nic curled them around his. He made another pass, this one just as slow and soft, his lips over hers. It had been a long time since she'd done this, but she couldn't recall the feeling of wild horses dancing on her chest before.

Her lips remembered their part, though, and suddenly, Nic realized she was kissing him back. Really kissing him. The lazy stroke of his tongue over hers was delicious and wicked, too, and Nic's body was warm now.

All too soon, he pulled away from her, but he held her eyes in his gaze.

"What—?" She cleared her throat, but the word still came out like a croak. "What was—?"

His smile was sweet, and the thought of those lips on hers just moments ago made her ache in places she'd thought were long dead. She flicked her gaze up to watch him as he reached to pluck something from her hair.

"You had," he shrugged, and Nic's eyes were drawn to his lips again, "mistletoe in your hair."

"Mistletoe?" she whispered, and her heart did a belly flop. She'd fallen for a moment. Believed in the magic of the season. When in reality, Scott had only kissed her because he was supposed to because of the mistletoe.

"Let's get new lights and start again tomorrow."

TWO

OH DAMN.

You just kissed her. You just kissed Nic Collier, you dumbass.

Scott Woodrow held his breath and waited for Nic to give it to him with both barrels. She didn't, though. In fact, Nic Collier—cool and collected under the craziest of circumstances—appeared flustered. She stared up at him —even on the first rung of the ladder, she was a bit shorter than him—with big, wild eyes. Reminded him a bit of Bambi, kind of doe-eyed innocence, and the thing was? He knew Nic well enough to know that low-key didn't necessarily mean innocence.

Grasping for something to make it okay—she wasn't his boss exactly, but they were coworkers and she had seniority over him and she kind of did boss him around and before that kiss, they'd bumped elbows a time or two hundred but never touched in a personal way—Scott snatched make believe mistletoe from her hair and offered her a small smile.

"You had mistletoe in your hair," he lied, and then immediately wished he hadn't.

The kiss was okay. Scratch that. The kiss was smoking hot. Even standing out here in the bitter wind with his balls freezing, that kiss with Nic had sent flames roaring through his blood. But the lie. The line about mistletoe. He shouldn't have said it.

Because Nic had kissed him back. She'd been startled at first, but she'd sunk into his kiss, his mouth, with easy, delicious surrender. The slide of her tongue against his was intoxicating. He wondered now if she felt it, too.

"Right." She nodded and cleared her throat.

Nic averted her eyes from his and blinked. She cleared her throat and then looked back up at the icicle lights hanging from her gutter. Half of them were lit, the other half dead. Scott had suggested new lights so they could get out of the cold for a few minutes. He wasn't a masochist, wasn't much of a shopper, but if strolling the Christmas aisles at the local discount hardware store meant getting out of the cold for a half hour, he was all in.

Besides, no way in hell she would win any contest— even one their station was sponsoring—with a half-ass light job.

"Nic." He stirred to life as she climbed back up the ladder. "Would you let me do that?"

"Nope." Her voice barely carried to him. Pint-sized, she looked like a kid up on the ladder, arms up over her head as she tugged the lights back down. Was it his imagination, or was she yanking them down with fervor? Come to think of it, she was muttering something, too, as she worked. Not sure if it was better to remain silent, he stepped into the landscaping—which could use some attention, too, he decided—and held onto the ladder to hold it still.

"Let me get the rest," he said as she came down the ladder again. She froze on the ladder when she backed up against him. Through two heavy winter coats and everything else the two of them wore underneath, it shouldn't have affected him.

"Scott—"

Any blood in his body that wasn't thick with cold rushed south when she didn't move. She looked over her right shoulder when she said his name. Scott dragged his eyes over her face, careful not to linger on her lips, and then took a step back and mentally counted to five.

"Why don't you go pick up some of the stuff in the garage? Make sure everything's locked up? I'll get the rest of these, and then we can go."

After having his offers to help turned down at least ten times, he fully expected her to argue again. When she didn't, when the only sound was the brisk wind stirring the bare tree limbs and the rattle of a loose drain pipe on a neighboring house, he tipped his head and studied her expectantly.

"*We* can go?" She met his eyes with a frown. He nodded uncertainly. "Why?"

"Why what?" He shook his head. His nuts were back to feeling frosty. Coffee sounded good. Strong, hot coffee. With a generous shot of whiskey. Or maybe just a generous shot of whiskey minus the coffee would do it.

"Why would you go with me?"

"Why wouldn't I?" he answered with a deep shrug. "Nic, I'm so cold I can't feel my—face." He nodded toward the garage. "Go lock up. I'll finish these."

She glanced back at the house but not up at the lights. Finally, she nodded and backed the rest of the way off the ladder. Ready for her this time, Scott made sure to step out of her way. He watched her for a second as she stalked back to the open garage.

Interesting.

He'd only known her for a year, but he wasn't sure he'd ever seen Nic Collier in a pissy mood like this. Sure, she got pissed at work. At people. At technology. At herself. And when she did, she let it rip, gave someone a little piece of her mind, and then she was over it. She wasn't one to stew, and Scott was sure this whole night had been one big bowl for her.

Before she could peek back at him and catch him watching her, he adjusted the ladder about a foot and a half to the right, made sure it was set firmly in the ground, and climbed up. Darkness crept in on him over here away from the bright glow of the porch light. Hanging Christmas lights was better suited to daytime work, but then it had probably been daylight when Nic started. Still, she was a stickler for efficiency and productivity, so it surprised him that she hadn't waited for a Saturday. By contest stipulations, she had over a week to get the lights up.

Scott pulled this strand of lights down and then glanced at the feet of the ladder dug securely in the ground. From the corner of his eye, he saw Nic moving around at the opening of the one car garage. She was tossing Christmas decorations haphazardly into a big green tub. Maybe he wasn't the only one who thought whiskey was a good idea. Rather than take the time to climb down and move the ladder again, he reached to the right and caught the white-coated wire with his finger-tips. The lights gave with his firm tug. Fingers a bit numb now, he hurried back down the ladder and gathered up the discarded lights.

He used to help his grandpa with Christmas lights. They always made a day of it. Grandma stuffed them with eggs and bacon and then sent them out to do the *men's work*, and then when they were finished, she would greet them at the door with hot cocoa for Scott and coffee for Grandpa. Cookies fresh from the oven were a staple. Until Grandma passed away. He and Grandpa had continued with the lights and the decorations—after all, there were seventeen other grandkids around during the holidays—but the cookies were no longer fresh from the oven.

Still, decorating for the holidays was one of his favorite things to do. He had the distinct impression that Nic wouldn't say the same. He found her squatting by the green tub when he took the lights to the garage. Hands on her knees, she shot him a guilty look, like he'd caught her doing something naughty, and then offered him a small smile. A bit more like the woman he knew, but still not totally Nic.

"Ready?" he asked hopefully.

"Yeah." She nodded and stood. "Here." She reached for the lights he carried. Scott handed them over and then headed back to the front to grab the ladder. He carried it around to the garage and set it down when Nic indicated it went on the south wall.

He pulled his keys from his pocket and arched his brows at her.

"Let me grab my keys," she mumbled. He nodded, but

rather than stand in the cold to wait for her, he climbed into his truck and started it.

What the hell?

Now that he was alone for a second, he had time to revisit that kiss. She was cute; hell, he'd thought she was sexy before standing at the bottom end of a ladder and watching her denim-clad butt move around all night. But they worked together. Workplace relationships were a definite no. So, what was it? Why had he just chucked the past year of working with her, of friendship, and his brain out the window to kiss her?

Because she looked so distraught. All night working on these damned lights, she'd looked so out of sorts. Still, it wasn't like he'd kissed her just to cheer her up. Scott dated enough, but he didn't see himself as some sort of hero who could swoop in and rescue a woman with a kiss.

Nope. Maybe it was just the mystery, the new side of her that he'd never really encountered. Had to be it.

The woman of his thoughts yanked the passenger door open and plunked him right back down in the truck with her. She hauled herself up to sit and then sighed. Scott shot her a look, but he couldn't decipher the look on her face.

"You okay?" he asked quietly.

When she only nodded, he dropped the truck in reverse and backed slowly from her driveway. The truck had some age on it, but the heater worked like a dream. For the first time since he'd arrived at Nic's a couple of hours ago, his nuts and his ass were finally thawing out. The temperature had taken a sharp drop the week of Thanksgiving, but thankfully, they hadn't had any snow yet. He could just imagine being out there with an angry Nic stomping around in the snow.

She clicked her seatbelt and then spent a few moments looking at her phone.

Cloquet was no *small* town, but on a random Thursday evening, traffic was light, and the drive from Nic's to Benson's Hardware took them less than five minutes. Unfortunately, Scott pulled into a parking lot as full as a car sales lot. He swallowed a groan as he swung the truck into a spot at the far end of the second parking lane. He'd offered to come with Nic; Hailey Gerristen's after hours summons be damned. He would survive a half hour in hell.

THREE

"REALLY?" NIC LEANED INTO HIS RIGHT SIDE TO LOOK AT the tacky Christmas wreath in Scott's hands.

"Pretty hideous, isn't it?" He shot her a grin over his shoulder.

"Mmm." She nodded and stepped away from him. Scott lingered there with the fake-looking pine wreaths, but she moseyed through the aisles until she found the lights. "Oh, man." She'd forgotten the variety in Christmas lights. So many shapes and sizes and colors to choose from. No wonder she'd gotten comfortable with the stupid icicle lights. Then again, she hadn't even put those up the past two years.

"If you can't find lights you like here, you must be a grinch." Scott's low voice rumbled in her chest as he sidled up beside her.

A little uncertain standing so close to him, Nic stepped away and shook her head. "Am I green?"

He laughed. "How long have you had the icicle lights?"

"I don't even know," she mumbled.

She knew. She and Pete had strolled this very aisle four years ago, hand in hand, to pick out lights and an artificial tree. Nic had been happy to let Pete make the decisions then, and she'd watched, amused, as he studied the different sizes and styles of lights like he would be tested on everything later, before choosing the icicles. They'd taken everything home and put the tree up in the living room, because it had been too late to start on the outdoor lights.

"Hmm." Scott folded his arms over his chest and rubbed his fingers over his lips. Nic looked away quickly, reminded of Pete, though really, they looked and acted nothing alike. "What do you like?"

A rush of heat flooded her face. Between the kiss earlier and now the memories of Pete and that Christmas when they'd bought the decorations and then got the tree and other things up, too, she couldn't spare Scott a glance.

"I don't know." She shrugged and then, remembering Scott had given up a free evening to help her out, she took a step closer to the lights and tried to concentrate. LED. Flashing. Musical. No. No way did she want anything that flashed. She didn't want her house lighting up the neighborhood like a strip club. No musical anything. That was more Callie's speed than hers.

"Okay." Scott stepped up beside her again. Nic hoped he didn't notice her flinch. The kiss was obviously nothing. Scott Woodrow wasn't hiding a long-lived crush. He wasn't dying to take her home and do it again. Nothing he'd ever said or done had given her that impression.

So, then, why had he kissed her? Sure, he'd used the mistletoe excuse. The thing was? Nic didn't have a bit of mistletoe anywhere in her admittedly small Christmas decoration collection. Which meant he'd lied. Fibbed. Whatever.

He bumped her hip with his and grinned when she braved a look at him.

"Want some direction?"

She did, yes, but she also wanted another taste of his lips on hers. Which was dumb. Because before that five seconds in the bushes on the ladder when he'd kissed her, she had never considered Scott as anything more than a friend she worked with.

"Please." She gave in with a laugh. "Pick something. Put me out of my misery." She swept her hand out to indicate the lights and then stepped back to let him do his thing. Were there really women who enjoyed this stuff? Not just the outdoor lights, but the whole Christmas kit and kaboodle?

Well, yes, there were; her mom and sister being two who had left a huge impression on Nic.

"Okay, do you like—"

"Scott," she groaned and shoved her hands in her coat pockets. When they'd walked inside, she had immediately tugged the zipper down, the heat from the store smacking her in the face. Now, though, she needed something to do with her hands. Pockets seemed like a good idea. Because if he asked more questions about the lights, she might slug him.

"Stay with me. Easy question," he promised.

"An easy question would be neat or on the rocks?" she argued.

He laughed; Nic noticed the way his eyes lit up with amusement. Dang. Had she ever seen that look on his face before? Was she making stuff up now? Was she reading something into the evening just because it had been a while since she'd even been kissed?

"Very true," he agreed. "What's your favorite color?"

She opened her mouth, but before she could speak, he held up a hand and shook his head.

"Don't say black," he warned her.

"Why would I say black?" She laughed, although she was a bit stung by his assumption. Did she seem like that kind of girl? Wasn't she too old to be into black? She'd never worn black lipstick or nail polish a day in her life, and though she wasn't Hailey Gerritsen—or Callie—she wasn't a cynic, either. At least, she didn't think she was.

Scott—turned back to the huge array of lights—must have felt her watching him, because the corner of his mouth tipped up in a grin. He shrugged, shot her a peek, and then looked away again.

"What is it then?"

"Blue," she answered simply.

"Okay. Do you want blue lights?"

She started to answer him, but this time, she cut herself off and stared at him silently.

"What?" Arms still folded over his chest, he turned to look at her. This time, he studied her intently, waiting for her to answer him.

"I don't. I don't know." She shrugged.

"You don't know?"

"No. I mean. Does it matter?"

"Nic." He groaned and shook his head, but she was relieved to see the smirk on his face. He might be amused by her, but he didn't appear to be put out that he was here with her and not somewhere—anywhere—else. He rolled his head on his neck and then hit her square in the pride with his bright blue eyes. "Okay. Let me ask you this."

"So many questions." She squeezed her eyes closed and pulled in a deep breath. "Okay. Hit me."

"When you're driving around, looking at Christmas lights, what do you like? Do you think the colored lights or white lights are prettier?"

Nic blinked her eyes open, but she only stared at him.

"These aren't hard questions," he reminded her.

But they were, for reasons she wouldn't get into.

She rubbed her lips together and glanced at the boxes and boxes of lights to her right.

"I don't drive around and look at Christmas lights," she admitted. "At least not on purpose."

When he didn't answer her, she chanced a quick peek in his direction. The intense blue of his eyes made her squirm.

"Just do white," she mumbled with a lazy shrug.

"Big or little?" he asked without fanfare. Nic watched him again as he swept his gaze over the Christmas merchandise.

"Big."

She had worked with him for a year—sometimes in close quarters, covering breaking news, hanging at the station for hours on end during severe storm coverages—and they were friends, but she didn't know him well enough to make a joke out of what he'd asked and she'd answered. In fact, at the moment, she felt decidedly serious and a little bit blue about the whole Christmas thing. She was ready to get this done and get home. Ready for him to be free of her and on to whatever Scott

Woodrow normally did on a random week night in early December.

"Now we're getting somewhere." He nodded. Nic watched him select several boxes of big white lights and stack them against his chest. She thought again of Pete, of the way he'd carefully selected the lights and the extension cords and the replacement bulbs and placed each item in the shopping cart with thought, as if something might explode if placed in the wrong position.

"You okay?"

Nic felt the frown on her face when she heard Scott speak. She made a conscious effort to smile when she looked at him, relieved again, when she found him smiling.

"Yeah." She nodded. "Is that all I need?"

"You might need some extension cords." He scrubbed his hand up over his sandy blond hair and then wrapped his fingers around the back of his neck as he looked down at the lights he held stacked against his chest and considered whatever things needed to be considered for outdoor holiday decorating. Nic swallowed an impatient sigh when she saw his booted toe tapping.

Now that was cute. Toe tapping while thinking.

"We'll start with this," he finally announced. "Not sure how many light sets we'll need. But once we get started Saturday, I'll be able to tell if we need more. You can bring one of the boxes out and pick up more if we do."

We. Saturday.

Tired and feeling guilty for keeping him, Nic didn't question his choice of words. No, Hailey hadn't said she couldn't enlist help for the contest. If she wanted to, Nic could get a crew of volunteer firemen over to do the house. Not that she knew any firemen. And not that she wanted to.

"Okay." She nodded and spun on her heel, ready to hurry through checkout and get back home. It was too dark now to do anything else with the lights, but she was ready to get home and set Scott free. She would find something on TV to watch or she would surf the Internet, reading news tidbits—gossip or real, though most things she read she attributed to the former.

Scott lingered, though, in the Christmas aisles. When she realized he wasn't following her, she turned and took a few steps backwards, surprised and amused to find him studying a life size Santa Claus.

"You still believe?" she asked and grinned when he gave her a sheepish look.

"You're never too old to believe in Santa Claus."

"Right." She nodded.

"My younger sister wrote a letter to Santa every year until she was thirteen."

"She did not," Nic argued.

"Swear!"

"What does a thirteen-year-old girl ask for?"

"Well, I don't know. That was twelve years ago. What was in for girls twelve years ago?"

Nic snorted and rolled her eyes. "I dunno. I was a tomboy."

"No frilly skirts and baby dolls for you?"

She flashed on the one baby doll she'd had when she was seven or eight. Nic had named her Debra, but she wasn't going to share that with Scott.

"No."

"I asked for sports stuff," Scott told her as he walked

toward her. They moved toward the checkout lanes, Nic relieved to see there were no long lines. Things would get nuts here in a few weeks, with the holiday shoppers descending on all the stores. "Until I was older. Then I started asking for camera equipment."

They stood in line behind a woman buying three bags of cat food. Nic eyed the bags and then the young kid at the register—three earrings and a tattoo of a dagger on the side of his neck—and then the woman buying the cat food. She didn't have a problem with tattoos, though she had none. Nor did she have issues with earrings, although she thought some were more attractive than others. This kid wasn't attractive, though. She guessed him to be a new sixteen, and he looked ill, he was so scrawny and pale.

He took the woman's cash and happened to meet Nic's gaze as he counted out change. The friendly smile spiked through her like a poisoned dart. Why was she standing here judging this kid because he was skinny? When had she gotten old?

Well, that was easy. She'd been old for a damned long time. If she wasn't careful, she was going to end up like the woman in front of her. Out in the evening buying cat food for entertainment. Nic had nothing against cats, but she didn't love them, either. And she really didn't love the idea of being an old single cat lady, which was unfortunate since she was already well on her way.

"So, when you were—how old?—you started asking Santa for sports equipment?" Nic dragged her eyes from the woman in front of her and twisted around to look at Scott.

Neck bent, eyes on a magazine in the counter rack, Scott grinned and moved only his eyes to look at her.

"I asked my parents for camera equipment," he clarified.

"Okay." She nodded and stepped up to the register when the other woman moved on. Careful not to topple the small pile of boxes in his arms, Scott stepped up beside her and started unloading the pile to the conveyor belt.

"What about you? What was your big thing you asked for for Christmas?"

"The big thing?" she repeated with a frown. "I dunno. I think I had an Easy Bake Oven when I was a kid."

"Do tomboys play with those?"

"Well, no, *I didn't*, but guys cook, so I think tomboys *can* probably cook and bake, too."

His grin was slow in coming this time, but while Nic waited for it, eyes on his face, she noticed the golden whisker scruff around his lips and over his jaws. It wasn't thick or dark enough to be terribly noticeable, though there were days when he looked a little rough around the edges. She decided she kind of liked the look, and she decided she would think that now even if he hadn't kissed her earlier. After all, he was just that good-looking. Every woman at the station coasted her eyes over him every chance they got, even Evelyn, the woman who cleaned the building, and she was old enough to be Scott's grandmother.

"And do you?"

"Cook? Or bake?"

"Either."

The kid at the register scanned the boxes and gave Nic a total, but he seemed more interested in their conversation than the debit card Nic swiped.

"Some."

"Man, I could go for some homemade brownies right now," the kid mumbled as he pulled the receipt from the printer and tucked it in one of the plastic bags. Nic flashed him a smile as Scott grabbed the bags.

"Me, too," Scott agreed. "Take it easy, man."

Nic zipped her coat as they neared the automatic doors.

"Want me to get the truck and pick you up here?"

Nic lifted her head and stared at Scott with disbelief. "Really? Did you just ask me that?"

He shrugged, but she caught the eye roll.

"It's cold, Nic," he reminded her.

"I can handle it."

"Oh, I know." He nodded. "I was just being nice."

She blinked at him as the doors opened, and they stepped outside. The cold wind hit her bare neck and then went down her back, under the loose long-sleeved tee she wore. She hid her shiver, though, in case Scott was looking.

"What next?" he asked as they neared his truck. The lot was still packed, and Nic decided they were lucky not to have stood in line. She wondered where everyone inside was, what they were shopping for. She needed to get her nieces and nephews gifts, but she usually sent gift cards, so there was really no rush. Still, the idea of having to brave crowds like this even to buy a gift card somewhere made her shudder. "Nic?"

"Nothing." She shook her head.

"You don't have anything to do now?"

She considered lying. Saying she had a lot to do, but nothing she needed help with. In the end, she only shook her head again. Why lie? Why lie to impress Scott now, after knowing him all year? Seemed silly, especially since he could call her out for being less than truthful, because odds were, he could catch her in a lie if he wanted to.

Then again, he'd lied to her earlier.

About the mistletoe.

And the kiss.

"Nothing on the agenda, other than some TV time, maybe."

He fished his keys from his pocket and aimed the fob at the truck.

"Wanna go get coffee? Before I take you home?"

FOUR

Rather than stand there and watch the range of emotions as they colored Nic's face, Scott pulled the driver's door open, tossed the lights on the floor in the middle of the cab, and climbed in. He caught the surprise on her face, but he knew there were all sorts of looks he probably missed. Dismay. Discomfort. Who knew?

Then again, they had just been teasing each other about Christmas and presents, so they were safely back in the friend zone. Not that they'd really ventured that far outside the zone. Friends kissed each other now and then, right? Especially when there was mistletoe involved.

Although, maybe friends kissed each other on the cheek. It was called bussing the cheek in Europe, he thought. Maybe not open-mouthed French kisses, although if he had to choose, he was a fan of the latter.

And also, there really hadn't been any mistletoe involved, but maybe Nic didn't know that.

"Sure."

Lost in his thoughts again, Scott hadn't paid attention

to Nic as she got in the truck, and her answer rendered him momentarily speechless. Maybe he should have suggested a bar. She'd referenced whiskey in the Christmas department inside, and they'd been out together with the crew on a number of occasions. Nic wasn't a partier by anyone's definition, but she appeared to enjoy hanging at the bar—Gin & Harry's—and having a drink.

Then again, maybe she enjoyed hanging at the bar with the rest of the crew. Might seem more like a date if it was just the two of them. Which, maybe, wouldn't be so bad. But would she think so?

"Something come up?" she asked when he still didn't answer her or make any move to start the truck.

"No." He grinned and stabbed the key into the ignition. She laughed softly when he looked at her. "I think I was just shocked that you said yes."

"What?" This time her laugh was louder, a little sharp around the edges. "Why wouldn't I say yes?"

"Well, I offered at least ten times to put your lights up earlier, and you said no at least as many."

"Eight, and that's different." She shrugged.

"How's it different?" He put the truck into gear and followed the marked path out of the lot and then turned right into the west bound traffic. Even though it was full dark now, it was only seven, so Scott steered the truck to a smaller, local bakery café rather than hitting the big dog just a block further down.

"I don't need help." She tipped her head at him. "I can deal with the house stuff."

He nodded as they left the truck and headed over the lot to the fancy café his sisters loved. Emily loved their coffee;

Megan loved their pastries. Unfortunately, according to her, she ate too many of them and was now fat. Scott thought she finally looked good and healthy. Megan had struggled a bit with an eating disorder when she was younger. Scott made a point of dragging her out to grab a bite to eat at least once a week, and though they did frequent the café, Megan usually insisted they find something healthy.

"I didn't say you needed help," he clarified as he pulled the door open for her. Inside, it appeared that Christmas had already arrived. Small, twinkling lights hung around the counter and from the wall behind the counter, which was laden with every sort of pastry and cookie and bread Scott had ever heard of. And several more.

"But Hailey suggested you swing by and help a girl out, right?"

Scott blinked at Nic's acerbic tone, but she stepped up to the counter and greeted the woman there by name. What was that all about? Hailey had told him Nic was planning to do her lights, but it wasn't like an order. Granted, Hailey had texted him, so he hadn't heard her voice to pick up on any sour tone. But he wasn't sure Hailey *had* a sour tone; she was cotton candy and bubble gum compared to Nic's no-nonsense black coffee.

"What'd you get?" He edged up to the counter beside her and tucked his hands in his coat pockets. Maybe to keep from snatching a pile of chocolate chunk cookies on the counter by the register or maybe to keep from nudging Nic. Because they weren't really the nudgy, touchy-feely kind of friends, were they?

Other than an hour ago when he'd had his mouth on hers and stuck his tongue in her lips and she'd stroked hers right back over his. That was something, although Scott couldn't begin to define it. And he wasn't willing to give it too much thought.

"Coffee." She looked up at him, any trace of that snippiness regarding Hailey long gone. Her eyes were a much lighter blue than his, but standing close to her now, he noticed flecks of deep, dark blue, also. The Christmas lights made her hair shine, and he could easily see a few chunks of platinum blond tousled through the reddish purple. "Black."

"Shocker," he only mouthed the word, but she read his lips. She laughed softly, but she elbowed him in the ribs. As short as she was, she was a long way from his heart, but he felt a stab of something there, anyway.

"And a cookie."

"Yeah?"

"White chocolate macadamia," she told him.

"My sister's favorite."

"The sister who wrote to Santa when she was thirteen?"

"Nope. That was Emily. Megan loves the cookies."

"How many sisters do you have?" Nic turned as if she sensed the woman behind the counter was there with her coffee mug. She took the mug and the small wax bag with a quiet thank you.

"Only two, thank God," Scott answered, dodging when she swatted at him. He ordered coffee and an oatmeal cookie and catalogued the movement when Nic turned up her nose. "What? They're a pain."

He flashed the woman a smile when she handed him a mug and his own wax bag, and then he and Nic wandered over to the counter at the east wall to fill their mugs. Nic eyed him curiously as he filled his.

"Decaf?" She lifted her full mug and sipped from it. "Really?"

"I don't sleep a lot." He looked around the café. Three tables were occupied up front, so he led Nic to a two-top by the windows. "Too cold?"

"No, it's warm in here." As if to prove her point, she tugged her zipper down and shrugged out of her coat. He watched her as she opened her bag to get her cookie. Her blunt cut nails were unadorned, but there was something magical about her hands. Maybe it was just that he'd seen her do so much in the studio—fingers flying over a keyboard, wrapped around a pen as she jotted notes for possible stories, adjusting lenses on the cameras for him, hammering nails into loose floor boards in the back room and tonight, dealing with the lights, determined somehow to make them work.

"Why do you hate Christmas?"

FIVE

NIC STOPPED CHEWING AND STARED AT SCOTT SILENTLY. Had he just asked her why she hated Christmas?

"I don't." She tried to swallow, but her throat was dry, and she had to sip her coffee to get the cookie down.

"You don't?" He tipped his head and arched an eyebrow at her.

"I don't love it, but I don't hate it."

"You had a murderous gleam in your eyes earlier dealing with those lights."

She snickered behind her mug.

"Just because I think Christmas lights are a pain doesn't mean I hate Christmas."

Scott narrowed his eyes at her and studied her face for a few moments. "Uh-huh."

"I hate being cold," she mumbled. Feeling chagrined, a little bit like he could see right through her, Nic lowered her gaze to the table and broke off another bite of her cookie. She shrugged and continued, "I'm not crazy about ladders."

"I offered to help you."

"You didn't, not really," she argued. "I know Hailey sent you over. I appreciate that you were there and offered to help, but—"

"But you don't ask for help."

Nic lifted her gaze to meet his eyes, popped the bite of cookie into her mouth, and shook her head.

"I don't mind lights. I just hate putting them up. I haven't…in…a few years."

Two, but that fell under things she didn't discuss.

"You don't mind lights, but you don't ever just drive around and look at them," he reminded her.

Nic watched as he pulled his own cookie from the bag and lifted the whole thing to his mouth to break off a big bite. Crumbs fell to the table, but Nic was more intrigued by the little crumbs that lingered on his lips. His words were a challenge, but she didn't care to rise to it. He was baiting her to talk about Christmas—or more to the point, what she had against it—and she refused to get into it.

"Um." She shrugged, eyes drawn to his mouth when he darted his tongue out to lick the crumbs from his lips. Unnerved by his action, she looked away and shook her head. "Just. I mean. Do people do that?"

Of course, people did that. Hadn't that been her mom and Callie's favorite damned thing to do on December evenings? Especially after Saturday evening masses? She and her sister would pile into the backseat of the car, her mom would turn on a traditional Christmas CD—Bing Crosby was her favorite—and her dad would cruise through the same neighborhoods, and they would all *ooh* and *ahh* over the same houses and the same lighting displays year after year.

"Yeah, people do that."

From the corner of her eye, she saw Scott nod.

"Okay, so what do you have against Hailey?"

That question caught her totally off-guard. She bit her lip as she turned to look at him. She could rattle an answer the length of a short novel, but she wouldn't. Wasn't her style to talk about people behind their backs. Besides, as much as Hailey Gerristen frustrated her, drove her up a frigging wall, she liked her. Most of the time.

"Nothing."

Eyes locked with his, she saw the disbelief and waited for him to challenge her. She held her breath, not sure if she wanted him to or if she wanted him to back down. No, she didn't want this coffee-thing to turn into a bitch session—about Christmas, Callie, or Hailey. But she was suddenly curious about him, about what he thought about things. About the holidays. Hailey. The studio.

She saw the moment he decided to accept her answer and let it ride. That intense flame in his eyes cooled a bit, and he turned his attention back to his cookie.

"Do you?"

"Do I what?" he asked her as he sipped his coffee.

She felt a grin at her lips when she realized she didn't know where she was going with that question.

"Like Christmas?" She tossed the words out on a whim.

"Love it." He nodded, and if the little spike of excitement in his voice didn't make the point, the twinkle in his eyes did.

"Still ask your parents for camera equipment?"

"No." His turn to grin. This one was a bit sheepish. "My parents don't get us gifts now. Maybe a gift certificate for dinner or movies or something. My sisters and I exchange names—"

"Really?" She tipped her head. When was the last time she and Callie had exchanged gifts? For that matter, when was the last time she and Callie had exchanged so much as a phone call?

"Yeah. That's usually the only gift I open on Christmas. Well, that and something from my godson. He's my nephew."

"How old?" She arched her brows, genuinely curious. She and Callie didn't often speak, but Nic was crazy about her sister's kids.

"That one is five," he told her. "Kristoff. My nephew Adler is three. And my nieces are two."

"Twins?"

"No. My sisters both have daughters who are two."

Nic snorted and looked away.

"What?"

When she only shook her head, Scott reached over the table and touched her hand. Nic catalogued the heat in his skin, filed away the little jolt of electricity she felt at his touch, and laughed softly.

"What?" He gave the back of her hand a squeeze.

Nic lifted her eyes to look at him.

"Do you see them often?"

"I do." Scott nodded.

"How was that? Two pregnant women in one family at the same time?"

With a defeated laugh, he sank back in his seat. Nic watched him move his hand, watched him rest it in his lap, and reminded herself that even if she hadn't sworn off men, they worked together, so this wasn't going anywhere other than coffee and cookies.

And Christmas lights.

"It was fun," he answered with a lazy shrug. "Most of the time. Things got dicey when they both wanted the last piece of pie or both needed to use the bathroom at the same time."

Nic laughed and shrugged her eyebrows. Callie had been a monster through three of her four pregnancies. She couldn't imagine if she'd had another sister who was pregnant at the same time. And no, it wasn't worth consideration that she could have been pregnant at the same time as Callie. For one thing, Callie would have come unglued. And another—most importantly—Nic had no desire to be pregnant. To be a mom.

And even if she did, she had to have a man around. At least for a few minutes. Hadn't happened yet. At her age, it didn't seem to be in the cards.

"What about you? Siblings?"

Nic opened her mouth to answer him, but she hesitated. It had been on her tongue to say no. No siblings. But she'd talked about Callie now and then—in very general terms—around her coworkers, so lying now would only beg the question why.

"One sister."

"And?" Scott picked up the last third of his cookie. "Are you close?"

"Not really," she answered quietly. She wasn't sure if she was lying, and it was a big, long story. She'd rather not bore the guy to death over coffee and cookies. After all, the news team needed a camera man, and besides, he'd offered to help with her outdoor decorating.

"Is she older or younger?"

"Two years younger," she answered simply. And then, deciding just to hit all the important things he might ask about, she continued, "She's married. Lives in the Chicago suburbs. Her husband is a lawyer. Working for partner at some big firm. She complains to my mom that he's never around, but somehow, he's managed to knock her up four times. And no, she's not pleasant when she's pregnant."

Scott blinked.

"I do, however, adore her kids."

"Okay." He nodded slowly. "Um."

She laughed softly. "Sorry. Kind of a sore spot."

"It's okay," he said quietly. "I understand."

SIX

FISTS TUCKED IN HIS POCKETS AND SHOULDERS HUNCHED UP around his ears, Scott stomped his feet and waited for Nic to open her door. Yesterday, a steel gray sky had spit some snowflakes, but the ground wasn't cold enough yet for it to stick. Today, though, the sky was the vivid blue of a painting, and the sun was so bright, the reflection of it off the white siding on some of Nic's neighbors' houses made his head throb.

The cold air—easily ten degrees colder today than it had been two nights ago—made his eyes water. He almost wished he wouldn't have said anything about tossing the old lights and starting over. They could be done by now. They could have finished the light job Thursday night, and he could still be warm and cozy in his bed.

Except then Nic's lights would look lazy and trailer park, and that was fine for some people, but it wasn't going to win her any competitions. And being that their news station was sponsoring the Christmas lights contest, and—more importantly—Hailey, the morning anchor, had challenged Nic on air, it seemed like a good idea for Nic to put a little effort into decorating.

And, he decided when Nic opened the door wearing loose-fitting, faded red pajama pants and a loose gray, long-sleeved pajama shirt—faded letters spelled the words *But First Coffee*—if they had finished everything Thursday night, not only would Nic's lights not look good, but he would have missed this moment.

Hair sleep-tousled and eyes squinted against the sunlight behind him, Nic blinked at him silently. She crossed her arms over her chest—maybe intending to hide the fact that she wasn't wearing a bra, but instead drawing attention to that very fact—and tipped her head.

"Scott?" She blinked at him.

"Can I come in?"

"What are you doing here?"

"At the moment, freezing my nuts off," he mumbled. The words were out before he could catch them. He shot her a quick look, relieved to see the smirk on her face. She took a step back to let him inside and then practically lunged at the door to shut the cold out.

"Okay, let me rephrase." She smiled sweetly, but he heard the note of sarcasm in her voice. "Why are you on my porch freezing your nuts off at seven in the morning on a Saturday?"

"Christmas lights," he reminded her with a shrug.

"Right." She nodded her agreement. "But not at seven in the morning."

"You're always up at this hour," he reminded her.

"Nope." She shook her head. "Not on Saturdays."

She lifted her hands now to push her hair from her face. The move exposed a sliver of skin between her shirt and pants. Scott's eyes roamed that sliver enough to memorize it—she had a small, flat mole on the left side of her belly button. Thoughts sliding too far down, wondering what sort of thing she might have on under the pj pants, he looked away, only to see the words on her shirt again. *But first coffee*. The shirt implied something else, after coffee. Probably something as innocent as opening presents, and yet, Scott could think of other fun things to do with her after coffee.

Today.

Any morning.

Every morning.

He cleared his throat.

"I got you out of bed?"

"Mmm." She nodded and rubbed her eyes.

"I'm sorry."

"It's okay." She shook her head and padded through the living area to the kitchen. Assuming he was supposed to follow her, Scott swept his gaze around the rooms in a search for knowledge about her. He'd known her for a while, really, as friends, but he decided now he didn't know nearly enough about her.

Like why her sister was a sore spot. And why she maybe didn't hate Christmas, but didn't seem to love it too much, either.

"I can come back later," he offered now. Standing in the kitchen, watching her go through the motions of making coffee felt too intimate. Scott couldn't help but notice the sway of her hips and every time her shirt slid up to expose skin.

"It's fine," she argued. "Just let me get dressed."

He nodded, though he was okay with her not getting

dressed just yet. A few more minutes of hanging out with Nic Collier in her pjs sounded just about perfect.

"Do you want some?" Standing at the sink, she held the glass carafe up and looked at him over her shoulder. "Or are you in a hurry? Do you have other things to do today? Scott, you don't have to do this. I talked to Hailey—"

"I would love some coffee," he interrupted her. Still looking over her shoulder, her eyes followed his hands when he unzipped his coat and shrugged out of it. "I don't have anything going on today, unless you count laundry. And what is it with Hailey?"

"What?"

"You said you don't have a problem with Hailey."

"I don't." She twisted around to gape at him innocently. "I don't have a problem with Hailey."

Before he could say anything, her shoulders drooped, and she hugged the carafe to her chest.

"I just." She cleared her throat and shook her head. "I don't expect you to do this. And I know she told you to come over here Thursday night."

Scott hooked his coat on the back of a chair.

"How do you know she told me to come over here?"

Did Hailey and Nic discuss it? Surely, Nic hadn't asked Hailey to direct him over to her house. And he hadn't noticed any tension in the studio yesterday between Hailey and Nic. Hailey had radiated her usual bubbly self. Nic had been in charge of the morning news meeting—bright-eyed and focused as she doled out story assignments—and quiet and focused through their live broadcasts. Business as usual.

"I just do." She rolled her lips inward, took a deep breath, and met his eyes. "I know I sound ungrateful.

Hailey can be a handful," she said quietly. "And I just don't want you to feel obligated to me because she pushed you into being here."

"Okay." He nodded. "Here's the thing. Hailey isn't my boss." He lifted a shoulder in a lazy shrug. "Yes, she can be a handful, and yes, she threw that challenge at you on air, and I figure there's more to it than her wanting you to represent the station in the contest. But I don't feel obligated to be here."

"You don't?"

"No. I like doing this stuff." He shifted his eyes away from her when he said that, because he'd like to do other stuff with her on a crisp, cold December morning, too, and looking at her and thinking about that might be a bad idea.

"You do?" She tipped her head.

"I used to help my granddad decorate their house," he told her. "And…"

"And?" Her eyes were wide with emotion, and while he'd like to think it was wonder or anticipation, he decided to error on the side of caution. He had been about to say *I like you*, but maybe that was too much, too fast. Maybe even for him.

"No other plans. I hate doing laundry."

Her lips curved up in a grin, but the smile didn't quite reach her eyes.

"Okay." She nodded. "Suit yourself."

He watched her walk through the last steps of making coffee. Lowered himself to sit at the table when she took a box of kids' cereal from a cabinet.

"Have you had breakfast?"

He grinned.

"If I say no, are you going to offer to whip up a bowl of tasty golden o's?"

She laughed softly. "I have eggs. And toast."

"I had eggs and toast this morning." He shook his head slightly and lifted his fingers from the table to wave her offer away.

"What time did you get up?" She put the box on the table and turned back to the cabinets to get a bowl and a spoon.

"Six, but I told you I don't sleep much."

"Why don't you sleep, Scott Woodrow?" She folded her leg under her as she slid onto the chair across from him. He watched her pour some cereal into the bowl and take a bite.

"You forgot the milk."

"I don't have any." She shrugged.

"Want me to go get you some?"

"No, thanks, I'm fine. I eat it this way most of the time."

He frowned and studied the back of the box.

"So?" Under the table, she nudged his leg with her foot. Scott resisted the urge to touch her, to take her foot in his hand, and run his thumb up under her arch. He gave himself a mental shake—where were these thoughts coming from?—and tried to focus on the conversation.

"What?"

"Why don't you sleep?"

"I never do." He shrugged.

"No deep dark secrets?" she asked with a grin.

"I'm an open book." He laughed. "If I get four hours a night, I'm happy."

"Hmm." She crunched a bite of her cereal and studied

him thoughtfully. "I thought maybe you had some skeletons in your closet."

"I hope that's not how you go about investigative reporting. Announcing that you're looking for skeletons."

"I haven't been a reporter in several years." She waved off his comment, still with the hint of a smile on her face.

"Did you start out in news? As a reporter?"

"I did." She nodded. "I love the news. Hated that part of it, though. Hated being in front of a camera. Hated being the one out covering things, especially in bad weather. Either it's hot and your makeup's melting off your face, or it's nasty and cold and your toes are going to fall off." She shrugged. "I like what I do now."

"Well, you're good at it," he announced. "So, why wouldn't you like it? Or is it that you like it, why wouldn't you be good at it?"

"Have you always wanted to be a camera man for the news?"

"No." He relaxed back in his chair. "I've always loved the camera. Being behind it, that is. I was a sports photographer for the paper before I started at the station."

"I knew that." She nodded. "You got some big shot at the state basketball final, right? The guys under the basket, the ball sailing through the hoop. I think Hailey said you could feel the net moving, the shot was so good."

Scott perked up at her words. Not the praise, exactly. But the fact that at some point, his name had come up between her and Hailey.

"I got a shot," he said modestly.

"So that's what you always wanted? To be a photographer?"

"No. I love it, but I wanted to make movies. I've put a few things together. Kind of…documentaries."

"Really?" She put her spoon down in her bowl and rested her elbows on the table. "That's interesting."

"Why?"

"What kind of documentaries?"

"Well, I did one on the civil war and my local community and how the war affected the community. How the people there contributed to the war effort. Looked at the artifacts the local history museum has."

"That's awesome. Where can I find it?"

"You can't."

"What? Why not?"

"It's all on my computer. Never got far enough to do anything with it."

"What's left to do with it?"

"Um." He shrugged, uncomfortable under her scrutiny. "Nothing, really."

"Scott!" She reached over the table as if to touch him, but sitting back in his chair as he was, she couldn't reach him. "Will you let me watch it?"

"No."

"Oh, come on."

The coffee maker chose that moment to beep. Scott sighed with relief at the rescue, though he feared Nic wouldn't leave it alone. She eyed him as she stood to pour their coffee.

"Okay. You tell me what you have against Christmas, and you can watch the documentary."

SEVEN

Nic snorted and nearly choked on a mouthful of dry cereal. She covered her mouth and stared at Scott silently. When he tilted his head and shrugged suggestively, she laughed again and shook her head.

"There's nothing to tell," she promised as she reached for her spoon again. Still struggling to swallow, she cleared her throat and patted her chest. "That game's not gonna work."

"What game?" Scott wagged his eyebrows. "I like games."

"You show me yours, I'll show you mine." The words nearly froze on her lips as she heard them as they might sound to him. Certainly not what she meant, but judging from the boyish grin on Scott's face, she knew what he was thinking. Ignoring the slight blush in her cheeks—she could feel the tingle in her skin—she rolled her eyes. "Not what I meant."

"And yet, still intriguing."

"What?" She shot him a peek when she heard him

mumble behind her. The picture of innocence now, he leaned forward, elbow on the table, chin resting in the palm of his hand.

"Word has it that Chuck Holt bought a tank." He tipped his head a bit as he spoke. Knowing Chuck Holt, Nic wouldn't doubt it if the guy bought a tank and had it covered in diamonds and pearls and drove it to work every day. She poured two cups and then carried them back to the table.

"He bought a Hummer," she corrected him. "I saw it yesterday."

Chuck Holt, their weatherman, had recently divorced wife number three, and Nic suspected he was now in pursuit of his fourth victim. The guy lived large and dazzled people with his possessions, because his personality couldn't get him through a door. She'd never been a fan of his, but he'd been at the station when the Pollman Group hired her, so she figured she was stuck with him until Chuck left on his own.

"When did you see it?"

"Stepped outside for a break." She slid back onto her chair.

"You smoke?"

"No." She shook her head. "Just needed some air."

"Interesting."

"How so?"

"You step outside for air when it's cold enough to singe your nose hair and make your lungs ache."

"It's not that cold yet." She favored him with another eyeroll. "Are you from the south?"

He rewarded her with a sloppy grin and that low,

rumbling laughter. He wasn't from the south, and she knew it, but she couldn't resist the barb.

"What color is it?"

"Gold," she answered, easily sliding back to talk about the Hummer. "Of course."

"Ever ride in one?"

"No." She sipped her coffee. "And no, I won't be asking for any rides in Chuck's, either."

"Probably wise," Scott agreed. "So, I take it this is the first year the station has sponsored a holiday lights contest."

"Yeah." She fiddled with her spoon again. She didn't particularly want to talk about Chuck Holt and his Hummer, but she didn't want to talk about Christmas, either. "For the last couple of years, we sponsored Christmas programs for local elementary schools. Pollman's got a lot of grandkids."

"That's what Hailey said."

Nic eyed him curiously, but she wouldn't ask. Not her business what Scott and Hailey discussed.

"I personally liked the concert series they did two years ago." She pushed her bowl away and relaxed in her chair. "Pollman worked with some local bands. They did concerts from Thanksgiving to Christmas. Proceeds went to the music program. He had some boy band come in for the big finale. It was a big deal."

"So I heard." Scott nodded.

Nic wondered if he'd heard from Hailey, but she bit her lip to keep from asking.

"How come they switched it this year? To a lighting contest?"

"Pollman says it's because he wants to inspire the

community to get in the spirit of giving and the holidays."
She shrugged.

"You sound less than inspired."

Nic chuckled. "I don't get the switch. It's not going to
bring in the money they're used to raising."

"The winner gets a pretty good chunk, though, right?"

"Yeah." She nodded. "And Pollman says he'll match the
winner's prize money in a donation to the local schools,
provided they use it for building upkeep and
maintenance."

"So, why aren't you out there leading the way with a
lighted torch? You could inspire thousands of people to
get involved."

"No one knows me, Scott. How am I an inspiration?
Besides, this is money out of Pollman's pocket, and I'm
hearing those pockets are only so deep."

"People know your face now," he reminded her. Nic
winced at the memory of Hailey flashing her headshot on
their live broadcast on the first of December, calling her
out and challenging her to participate in the Christmas
lights contest for the good of the community.

"What would you do with the money if you won?"

Nic sighed and shrugged her lips in thought. "I don't
know. I could use it around here, for sure." She hadn't
done much in the way of upkeep around her own home
since Pete left. She hadn't done much in the way of
upkeep for herself, either, since Pete left. She could start
with simple things like landscaping for her yard and a spa
and facial treatment for herself. And wrap it up with new
paint and flooring in the house.

"Donate it to the schools," she answered simply.

"Liar."

"I don't need it."

"Everyone needs it, Nic. Everyone can use some extra pocket change, and that's a hefty bit of pocket change."

Nic offered him a lazy grin and pulled in a deep sigh.

"What would you do with it?"

"Frame some of my photography. Put a new central air unit in my house."

"Then maybe you should do this instead of me."

"No one knows me. And Hailey challenged you. Not me."

Nic rolled her eyes again, but this time she wasn't feeling fun or flirty. "Let me go get dressed, and we can get this done."

EIGHT

SCOTT CARRIED THE LADDER OUT TO THE YARD FULLY intending to be the one to do the climbing today. He rested the ladder against the side of the house and stood for a moment, head back and eyes on the roofline. Nic's little bungalow had two dormer windows begging for attention. Judging from the way she'd gone about the lights two nights ago, she had no intention of doing anything extra, nothing fancy.

He wanted to go fancy. Maybe not because Nic needed the prize money. But because Nic seemed to need the effort and maybe a win. Maybe because even though she denied it, he sensed something deeper than a simple holiday decorating contest between her and Hailey. He liked Hailey; he wasn't sure anyone *disliked* her, but that didn't mean he wasn't ready to be all in for Nic.

"What's wrong?" she asked as she joined him at the foot of the ladder. Zipped up now in her navy winter coat, she'd traded in the sexy, sleep-tousled look for cute. And he knew if and when he suggested what he was thinking,

she was going to get spunky. He fought a grin as he realized he was looking forward to it.

"Nothing's wrong." He shook his head and shifted his
eyes from her and back to the roofline.

"Why are you looking at my house like it's about to
collapse?"

"Nah, the house is sturdy." He folded his arms over his
chest and tipped his head, eyes still on the dormer
windows. "You could use some work on the gutters, but
the house is good."

When she didn't say anything, Scott chanced a quick
peek. Her eyes were already narrowed in concentration,
her lips screwed into a spunky, argumentative twist.

"So. You wanna have a go at some home improvement
here? Before hanging the lights?"

If he wasn't already cold, the nip in her voice would
have made him shiver.

"No." He shrugged, hoping he hadn't offended her. Her
house had good bones; it just looked a little lackluster and
sad. Since Thursday night, he decided she and her house
had something in common. He might never have noticed
the inherent sadness in her if he hadn't gotten tangled up
in the light project. "I'm just thinking."

"Yeah?" She jammed her hands in her coat pockets and
looked up at him. "And how are your nuts right about
now, Scott? Because I got some things pretty damned cold
here."

"Least your things are bundled up in a coat," he
reminded her. Their eyes met, and the quick flicker of a
grin over her face was almost more of a turn on than the
thought of her *things* getting cold. "Have you considered
putting lights on those dormer windows?"

When his suggestion was met with silence, he steeled himself for her argument and turned his head to look at her.

"No. I haven't." She shook her head. "Pete suggested it, but we didn't—we just. We never—the icicle lights." She shrugged and turned her nose up.

"Who's Pete?" His voice was dead quiet in the still morning. He hoped Nic hadn't heard the edge; he had no right to be jealous of some guy named Pete.

Except he was. Because if she had some guy named Pete, why wasn't he here with her? Why wasn't Pete helping her with the holiday decorating? And if she did have a guy named Pete who wasn't here helping, what the hell was that about? If Nic Collier was his, he would have started this morning a little differently—checking out some *things*—before they had morning coffee, and then he'd be helping her decorate the hell out of her house.

"Um." Nic blinked at him and opened her mouth to speak. Eyes wide with what appeared to be horror, she nibbled on her lower lip and finally shook her head. "He's my...ex." She looked away. "We bought the icicle lights together."

Scott dragged his eyes up to the roofline again and mulled that over. Nic and Pete had shopped together for icicle lights. And they'd probably done other stuff together, if he was her ex, because that implied that at one time, he was her everything, and now Pete was gone. Had Nic given him the boot? Or had he left her?

Did she still love him?

Is that why she hated Christmas?

Questions raging, afraid that he would sound like an

ass if he put a voice to any of them, Scott swallowed everything and nodded as he surveyed the roofline again.

"I think we should go big," he told her. "We could outline the whole face of the house. Dormers. The front door. The roofline. Even the pitch. Get a lighted Santa for the porch. Maybe even some reindeer for the yard—"

He stopped talking when he felt her eyes on him.

"Who are you, and what is this about? Hailey threw this at me on a live broadcast just to mess with me. I don't do Christmas like this, Scott. I don't want to."

"You don't want to?" He turned to her now. The wind whipped up and bit the exposed skin of his face. "Or you're afraid to?"

"What does that mean?"

"Hailey challenged you." He shrugged. "Don't just react. Take her on. Go big." Nic stared at him with those same wide eyes, only this time, Scott saw the little girl she would have been when she was a tomboy at home, ignoring her Easy Bake oven. "Have fun with it."

Nic huffed out an irritated sigh. "It's not fun."

"You're not having fun with me?" He threw his hand up over his heart and feigned chest pain.

Nic snorted and then cut loose with a big, long groan.

"When you were a kid," he started. She zeroed in on his face, the heat in her gaze warming him from the inside out. "And you didn't use your Easy Bake oven, what did you play with?"

"I don't see what—"

"Nic." He tipped his head.

"Basketball. I loved basketball. I shot baskets every day. Even when it was so damned cold, the ball didn't bounce right."

He studied her face a moment longer and then turned back to the house.

"I just think the face is great." He shrugged. "The face of your house. And it's perfect for lights. Symmetrical. The new lights you picked out will be perfect."

"I didn't pick them out," she reminded him. "You did."

"With your direction."

"She has an agenda," she mumbled. "And I don't wanna be a piece on her game board."

"So, what you're saying is that your refusal to get excited about this Christmas lights challenge is…political? Or does she have a personal vendetta against you? The bubbly blond anchor our world loves has something personal against you?"

Nic refused to look at him.

"What is it?" His voice was gruff. The agenda excuse was just that. Scott loved Christmas, and he did believe Nic's house was perfect for lights, and he could envision everything he'd described to her. But at the moment, he wanted to push through the bullshit and find out what really made this woman tick.

If they were at work, she might tell him to go to hell. Write him up. Send him packing.

But they weren't. They were in her front yard, and Scott found himself fighting the impulse to drag her into the garage and kiss that forlorn look off her face.

"What's what?"

"Hailey's agenda. What's her agenda?"

She'd buckled her emotions down in the space of a few seconds, and now she lifted her chin and met his gaze with cool indifference.

"I don't know," she said quietly. "But I don't want to be part of it."

"You already are part of it," he argued. "That's what I'm trying to tell you. So why not jump all in and enjoy it? The Nic Collier I know doesn't half-ass anything."

"You don't know me, Scott." She shook her head. "And don't do that."

"Don't do what?"

"Dare me. Don't add your own damned dares on top of hers."

"Okay." He held his hands up in surrender. "We'll do a straight line over the front of the house and be done."

Neither of them moved, except to look at the house instead of each other.

"I'll get the lights," he announced. "We should've…" He trailed off when he realized she wouldn't care if the lights were straight and evenly spaced.

"Should've what?" She followed him into the garage. Scott rubbed his hand over his face, feeling the bite of the wind even now.

"Nothing. Are the lights out here? That we got Thursday?"

"Should've what?" she asked again as she crossed the garage to grab the boxes. She'd backed her Toyota out of the way and parked it in the drive, and now she stood in the center of the stall, boxes stacked against the front of her zipped coat, and stared at him.

"Clips. We should've bought clips to space the lights out and keep them straight."

"What's in this for you?"

He dropped his head back and barked a sarcastic laugh. "I wonder."

She shrugged dramatically when he looked at her again.

"I don't know. I like Christmas," he said again. "I like a job well done. I'm a perfectionist."

She stared at him silently for a moment. "And if I win? You want half the money?'

"Yeah." He nodded as he stalked toward his truck in the drive behind her car. Frustrated with Nic and her cagey attitude and irked at himself for being intrigued and attracted and interested, he yanked the driver's door open and grabbed his work gloves from the front seat. His hands already ached from the cold. Nic was still in the center of the garage watching him when he turned around and swung the door closed. He intended to take the lights from her, but she stepped back and studied him with narrowed eyes. "Yeah, I'd take half of your money and donate it to the schools." His voice was thick with sarcasm.

Nic frowned, but she didn't answer him.

"I like you, Nic," he admitted. "I like being here. Yes, Hailey texted me Thursday to tell me you were planning to hang your lights. Nothing in her text suggested to me that she'd ask Pollman to fire me if I didn't show up. She didn't offer me any personal favors if I came here to help you. I still have the text on my phone if you want to see it."

"I don't wanna see it," she mumbled.

"I like you. I had fun Thursday. I even had fun shopping with you, and that might be the one thing about the holidays I don't like. I enjoyed the coffee date after shopping."

"That wasn't a date," she argued.

"Whatever." He tossed his hands up in frustration.

"Scott—"

Apparently, the cold had damaged his brain, because suddenly his hands were cupped on her upper arms, so he could haul her up to press his lips to hers. At least he had the will power to keep his tongue to himself this time. Her lips were warm and soft, and she smelled like coconut and coffee. She drew in a sharp gasp when he eased her back from her tiptoes to her heels. He peeked at her, and damned if he wasn't thrilled to see her eyes closed.

"I don't have mistletoe." She rubbed her lips together and blinked her eyes open. The ice blue drilled right through him.

"I lied." He shrugged. "Gimme the lights."

"I'm not gonna win." She tipped her head. Her arms flexed under his hands, but she only stuck her fists in her pockets. "I can't win. I represent the station, so I can't win a contest the station is sponsoring. You get that. Right?"

"You get how bad it'll look for the station if you don't do this? If you aren't excited about it? Not to mention the people that will rib you, personally, for hating Christmas."

"And you're still gonna donate your time to help me?"

"It's a real pain in my ass, but yeah, I'm gonna donate my time to help you do the lights. In fact, you can go back inside and do whatever it is you do on the weekends, and *I'll do* the lights. Would that make you happy?"

"No." She stepped back.

"Nic."

"I'm not gonna hang out inside while you work." She cleared her throat. "So. The clips. Can we get those at Benson's?"

"Probably."

"Wanna go shopping?"

NINE

Scott was right; Nic was an early riser. She had to be for her job. On a week day, she was usually in the studio just after five in the morning. She didn't go in on the weekends, but she was usually awake by six. That didn't mean she was ready for the doorbell at seven on a Saturday morning, though. In fact, she'd lain in bed for several minutes after she heard the bell, trying to decide if she was dreaming or if someone was, indeed, at her door.

To say finding Scott Woodrow on her front porch was a surprise would be an understatement. Honestly, she hadn't been sure he would come back to help with the lights, once he escaped her the first time. She figured he'd had a little shot of crazy with his coffee and decided to move right along. So, the fact that he'd come over at all was a surprise. That he'd shown up bright and early and then sat with her in her kitchen while she ate breakfast—in her pajamas!—had thrown her yet again.

And now this. Not so much that he wanted to make

the lights thing a big to-do, but the other stuff he'd said. *He liked her.*

What did that mean? He considered her a friend? Because that was okay; she'd always considered him a friend. She tended to look at the whole crew as friends rather than coworkers, even though technically as the news producer, she was their supervisor.

That's what he meant, Nic, she told herself. He considered her a friend, so of course, he wanted to come over and hang out with her and help with the lights. And yes, he was right. With the station sponsoring the Christmas lights contest this season, if the community got wind of her attitude about the lights or the holidays in general, there would be repercussions. And their competition, CCNO, would crush them in ratings, the station would lose advertising money and possibly credibility. CBTV wasn't in danger of closing its doors tomorrow, but Nic often heard tales of money being stretched thin due to certain deals and acquisitions and consumer support. She didn't want to be responsible for the Pollman Group and CBTV losing any funding.

So, yes, when Hailey Gerritsen had thrown that challenge at her the other night at the end of the evening news, Nic had been stunned. She liked Hailey; no lie there. But liking the girl didn't mean she had to trust her, and she didn't. The blonde had favored Nic with a grin and a head tilt and those sparkling blue eyes as she'd looked at her—off set, of course—and called her out by name and wondered if she'd be up for doing the CBTV Christmas Light Challenge. Speechless for a moment, because *Nic* wrote the broadcasts and that wasn't on the script, she'd stared at Hailey and even tapped her headset, to make sure it was working. To make sure it wasn't some horrid daydream or more accurately, nightmare. But the rest of the crew had all turned to her with silent thumbs up, and Wyatt Coben—Hailey's sometimes co-anchor— had drilled her with his big eyes and smile and a sloppy nod, and that was that.

Okay. She had to do the damned lights, and Scott was right about being lukewarm about it, too. So, she would go all in. She hadn't lied; she wasn't into driving around at night and looking at lights. No looking in big bay windows at warm holiday scenes or glowing Christmas trees and wondering what sort of family lived there. No warm fuzzies over pretty light displays in yards or around gated communities. She didn't know what was popular, what looked good, so she would happily give Scott the lead.

And not compare him to Pete Valenta.

Pete wasn't a bad guy; he just wasn't for her. They'd tried, and they'd both finally admitted they were bored with each other, and their boredom made them lash out at each other over silly things, like spacing ornaments right on the tree, as well as the big things. His favorite thing to do was poke at her with snide comments about her job, that with her cute, impish smile she should be in front of the camera, so a man could do the real work, gathering the news and writing the broadcast scripts and so on. Nic equated the barbs with Pete patting her on the head and telling her she was cute.

Pete owned a garage. He was a successful business manager as well as a good mechanic. Nic was thrilled for him. But she'd decided a long time ago—when she was still living at home with her parents—that she would never be the kind of woman to sit back and rely on her smile to get her places. She wasn't much of a kitchen type, much less a barefoot-and-pregnant-in-the-kitchen type, and Pete's comments had finally worn her down until she'd asked him to move out.

She missed him, but mostly she missed the company after a long day at work. She missed someone to laugh at TV sitcoms with. She missed sharing coffee in the morning, coffee, breakfast, and the newspaper on weekends, and she missed sex. Just not exactly sex with Pete.

"Everyone in Cloquet is here," Scott grumbled as he eased his truck into a parking spot in an adjacent lot. Cloquet Chiropractic and Sports Medicine was closed on Saturday, so Benson's shoppers spilled into their parking lot when necessary. Nic eyed the long walk to the doors and then shot Scott a quick frown. It was on the tip of her tongue to tell him they could just skip it, but as if he sensed it, he put the truck in park and turned to her with a boyish grin. "Ready for this?"

She might have agreed to do the lights and do them big, but she still found it hard to bubble with enthusiasm. Then again, that had always been Callie's department. Still, she mustered up a smile and a nod, and without a word, popped her seatbelt and opened the door to slide out.

Friends, she could do. She didn't mind the idea of getting to know Scott Woodrow better. Even if it meant hanging lights and garland and putting up resin Santas or snowmen or what have you. But friendship didn't address the kiss, did it?

Kisses, she corrected herself. Only one kiss had been intimate, involving a long, slow slide of tongues, but there had technically been two kisses. And a lie. And the confession of the lie upon confrontation. Did that mean anything? Any of it? Was she obsessing over nothing? Because even before Pete, she'd been the kind of girl to tiptoe into dating and relationships. She'd never been a third date sex girl; kissing friends—intimately kissing friends—was not something she did. Ever. But, Scott seemed unaffected by it. By any of it. Most especially the kiss itself.

On the other hand, he was the one who had kissed her. *Both times.*

"What?"

Nic looked up when he nudged her in the side with his elbow. The skies were so heavy with clouds, she hoped that didn't mean snow. If there was something she disliked more than Christmas, it was snow. Her luck, Scott was probably part Eskimo or had some distant relative who lived in Alaska. He might suggest building an igloo in her backyard once the Christmas lights were done.

"What?" She shook her head when their eyes met.

"You have this look on your face."

"What look?" Nic paused as a young kid in a green vest walked by her, pushing a train of carts. She blinked in disbelief. "Good grief. He's out for carts this early?"

"Well, technically, it's not that early anymore," Scott reminded her. "Black Friday's already over. Christmas shopping, Nic. Game on."

"Right." She nodded, but she still felt dazed. She generally did her shopping online or bought gift cards early. Rarely did paper and bows; if she needed something wrapped, she went with gift bags and stuffed tissue paper in the tops to make them look festive. Even though nine times out of ten, the results were pathetic, the tissue crinkled, and the corners of the bags themselves looked bent and soft.

Wow. Nic nearly missed a step as she walked beside Scott. She wasn't a woman anymore, at all. She didn't wrap presents, but she used to. Back in high school. For her besties when they did gift exchanges for birthdays or holidays. She used to wear makeup, now she usually limited her mirror time to fluffing her hair and swiping on mascara. She owned a good ten pair of jeans, but no dresses. She shaved her legs weekly. Sometimes. And she disliked Christmas and shopping.

"You look like you're trying to solve the problem of world peace," Scott told her as they stepped inside the store. Immediately hit with the wall of manufactured heat, Nic tugged her gloves off and unzipped her coat.

"Trying to solve a mystery," she mumbled and realized too late that she'd actually said the words out loud.

"Yeah? What mystery?" He flashed her a grin. "I'll help. I beat my sisters at Clue every time."

"Brag much?" She tipped her head and stepped around a group of teens gathered by a DVD display. She took a peek, not surprised to see that the movie they were all clambering for was a horror movie. She held her breath as she turned back to Scott and followed him to the holiday decorations. She had no intention of telling him she was pondering the mystery of Nicole Collier. She didn't want to admit that she'd been disillusioned with life when she was younger and so swallowed down all the tiny little bits and pieces that made her a happy, normal woman—then girl. She liked who she was now; this wasn't a sudden crisis where she realized she didn't like who she'd become. But seeing herself through Scott's eyes was new.

She was Nic Collier, tough, fair, and independent. All well and good. But she was more. There was a lot more inside that she'd tamed and hidden away. Funny that it took walking into Benson's with a work friend to realize she missed some of those things she'd wanted to deny herself years ago.

"So?" Scott tried again.

A work friend that had kissed her.

Twice.

The first of which had been smokin' hot and warmed her frozen toes and fingertips outside on an early December evening.

And apparently woke something feminine deep inside.

Not that she could tell him that, either.

"Why people are so enthralled by twinkling lights."

"Hmm." He studied her with a pensive look, which made her snort and roll her eyes. When he turned to head down the aisle of lights yet again, she followed him. She watched him expectantly, though, because she had no intention of giving him a pass on the mystery she'd fibbed about. Maybe it was dangerous to push him, because the twinkling lights and their fandom—though mysterious— was just a drop in the bucket compared to all the things on her mind at the moment. What if he dug a little more to uncover what she was really thinking?

Her belly flip flopped at the thought. Nic rubbed her damp palms on her jeans, and then it hit her. She was fidgety and nervous; she was pushing him because she liked him right back. She was *flirting* with him. Flirting. Just another of those things she'd shoved away and forgotten how to do when she was younger. She hadn't even flirted with Pete. They were friendly. They dated. They had sex. And eventually, they moved in together. And eventually, she'd asked him to leave.

This—whatever this was—was decidedly different.

"So? Got it figured out yet?" She stood at his elbow as he examined the same wall of boxed Christmas lights they'd looked at just the other night.

"Hmm?" He turned to her for a second, seemingly uninterested, and looked back at the lights.

"The mystery of the twinkling lights."

"Sounds like we're discussing Nancy Drew." He grinned and fixed his eyes on her again.

"I loved Nancy Drew when I was younger." The words gushed out before she could stop them. She felt her cheeks flush when Scott's eyes roamed over her face and lingered on her mouth.

"My sisters did, too." He propped his hands on his hips and turned back to the lights.

"You have no clue what the answer is, do you?" She tipped her head, shocked to realize she was enjoying herself. Egging him on. Flirting. This time, Scott twisted and angled his entire body her way and narrowed his eyes at her.

"I do," he answered with a nod.

Nic held the eye contact, her stomach poised and ready to fall, as if her toes were on the edge of a cliff, rather than in her scuffed brown boots, wedged right up against Scott's toes, hidden in gray athletic shoes.

"Enlighten me." She shrugged her shoulders as she took the plunge, and her stomach and her lungs and her heart flipped.

Her heart? *What?* Her heart had no business getting involved in any of this.

"The appeal of Christmas lights is much too personal and subjective to define in a general sense."

"Bullshit." Nic coughed and covered her mouth.

Scott's eyes flashed, but it was his grin that sent a shiver up her back.

"I can't give you a broad, generalized answer, but I can do something even better."

"Yeah? What's that?"

A harried-looking mom pushed a cart with a toddler in it past them, two more little kids hanging on her legs. She met Nic's eyes for a second and offered her a tired smile. Nic returned it, but the woman's bloodshot eyes and wrinkled blouse made her think of Callie.

Nothing was shivering on her now. No tingling. No flipping stomach, let alone heart.

"I'll show you."

TEN

THIS TIME WHEN THEY LEFT THE STORE, THEY HAD ENOUGH holiday décor to light up Nic's neighborhood. Scott didn't intentionally push her to do more; he got carried away. He'd told Nic about all the years he and his granddad had done the lights at the house, that even as he got older, he still loved to help. His younger cousins loved to see their grandpa's house done for the holidays, so he still climbed a ladder and walked on Granddad's roof to make sure the house looked festive.

Something had happened in the parking lot on the way in—something in Nic's head. She'd almost been a bit flirty for a few minutes. But then something else had happened in the holiday department—again, apparently in Nic's head—and she'd backed down a bit. But she'd still listened to his memories when he shared them. She'd offered her condolences when he mentioned that his grandma had passed away. She'd bit her lip and given up and laughed when he told her about Oscar, his grandparents' mutt, dragging a box of lights away from the ladder and back to his doghouse. She'd argued, called him on it when he told her he and his sister Emily had decorated Oscar's house, too, that year. She demanded proof, so he promised he would dig up pictures to share. It had been years ago; Scott was probably only fourteen or fifteen at the time, so it wasn't like he could whip his phone out and scroll through the photos to find one.

He'd decided if she balked at the money spent on the lights and clips and other porch and lawn decorations, he would pay half of it. After all, if she really hated Christmas and he had guilted her into going whole hog, he owed it to her. She didn't, though. She handed over her card and signed the screen at the register without blinking. As they piled back into his truck, he decided to buy her dinner.

Not like a date. He wouldn't ask her out and make a big deal of it. Something told him that might backfire. She might panic if she thought he was pursuing something more than a friendship born of the need to protect the station's pride and coffers. She might tell him no and that might be the end of it.

It. Whatever it was.

Scott snuck a look at Nic as he pulled the truck out into westbound traffic again to head back to her house. Head turned to stare out her window, he took a moment to appreciate the curve of her neck, the delicate shell of her ear where she'd tucked a chunk of hair back, and her hands, folded in her lap.

When she moved—just a tiny turn of her head—he looked back at the road, unwilling to be caught checking her out.

Maybe after they got the lights done, they could go get a pizza. Or order in. Well, no. That might not be a smart idea. Scott wasn't sure how he'd sat in her kitchen with her this morning while she ate breakfast and not made a fool of himself. Women, sleepy and warm, with their hair tangled and messy and their bodies clad in pjs, were incredibly sexy, and Nic had been no different. Scott loved the wild flip of her hair on the right side of her face. The line over her cheek where her sheet or pillow had marked it. The little glimpses of skin between her top and bottom, depending on how she moved. The loose sway of her breasts under her pajama top.

It was almost sexier than seeing her naked.

Well, no, not true.

He lifted his ass now and dropped a hand to adjust his dick while she wasn't looking. The only thing sexier than seeing Nic Collier naked would be touching her naked skin and lying between her smooth thighs and burying himself as far inside her heat as he could get.

The thought sending his dick right back to bursting, he muttered a string of curse words and then added a few more when she turned her cool blue eyes to him.

"What?"

He shook his head, all the while praying she didn't notice his erection.

"Do your sisters still live around here?" she asked him out of the blue.

"Within fifty miles." He nodded. "Emily just moved into a farmhouse in Angwin."

"Why?"

He couldn't ignore the horror in her words, nor did he miss the whole-body shudder.

"What do you mean?" he chuckled. "What's wrong with Angwin?"

"Um. Population fifteen?" Nic shot him a look that seemed to say *are you nuts?* "Oh. Sixteen if Emily now lives there."

"Her husband's a farmer," Scott told her. "Actually, his family owns half the town."

"So, like four cows and ten acres and a grocery counter?"

"Not a fan of small towns, huh?"

When he looked at her this time, she grinned.

"You prefer the big city life?"

"Not really," she answered. "I like visiting Chicago. I'd never live there."

"Megan lives here in Cloquet."

"Do you see her often?"

"Yeah. We go out for dinner once a week or so."

"Is she married?"

"No." Scott looked back at the road. He felt a tiny little tug at his heart and tried to push it away. Megan might never get married, because she was searching for something impossible to find. Her perfect man changed daily, and Scott suspected it was because she didn't know what or who she wanted, because she still wasn't happy with who she was. "Meg's a hard nut to crack."

From the corner of his eye, he saw Nic raise her eyebrows, but she didn't comment.

"And if I talked to either Emily or Megan, they would corroborate your story about decorating Oscar's doghouse?"

The laugh that rumbled up from his belly surprised him so close on the heels of the worry for his sister.

"It's not a story," he insisted.

She shook her head, but she was smiling, and inspired

by the smile, Scott turned the radio on. Johnny Mathis filled the truck cab with holiday music.

"Johnny Mathis," he told her.

"I know who Johnny Mathis is." She rolled her eyes.

"Yeah?" He shrugged a shoulder and pursed his lips. "Because you know, you don't do Christmas lights."

"Well, I am now, right?"

He finished the drive without further conversation, and then once he parked in Nic's driveway, he was ready to get to work. Nic opened the overhead garage door again and then tossed the remote she'd been carrying on the dash of her car. Scott went after the ladder again and made sure its feet were solid in the ground at the north end of the house.

"So, what do I do, boss?" Nic asked as she waited for him to finish studying the roofline yet again. Scott laughed softly and shook his head. "First, I need the clips. They'll hold the lights in place and that'll give them a straight, well-spaced look."

"Gotcha."

"And then we'll do the lights. I bought enough to do the pitch in the roofline and the dormers, too."

"Of course, you did," she mumbled as she walked away from him.

"Nic?"

"I refuse to put fake snow in my window panes." She stopped walking and turned to look at him. The smirk on her face hit him everywhere at once.

"That's so yesterday." He shook his head.

She mumbled again, something that sounded like *tell me about it*. He didn't ask her to repeat herself. Instead, he took the plunge.

"When we're done here?" Standing sideways at the ladder, he nodded to the house. "Wanna grab pizza or something?"

She stared at him for a few moments—long enough to make him sweat, and that was saying something, with the temperature hovering near freezing—and finally shrugged.

"Sure."

Stunned by her answer, Scott stared after her for a moment, eyes taking a trip down over her backside. Couldn't see much of her, bundled up as she was in the winter coat, but it was still a nice sight. He rolled his eyes as she disappeared around the corner of the garage.

What the hell was up with this sudden fascination with Nic Collier? They'd worked together for a year. He'd noticed she was cute; she was fair on the job and easy to work for. She was fun and easy going when the crew went out after hours. End of story.

He'd never entertained thoughts of any sort of fling with her. No sexy fantasies or dreams. No crushes or thoughts of getting to know her better.

Then again, he'd never spent any one on one time with her, either.

So, what, Scott? You're hot for her after hanging out with her for a couple of hours? Well, yeah, that part was believable. What guy wouldn't be hot for her after getting up close enough to see the flecks of dark blue in her light blue eyes? Or watching her ass for hours on end while she was up on a ladder? Or kissing her and that zing! of electric energy in his blood when she kissed him back?

Okay, easy to follow that part. On set at work, Scott had never had the time to study her the way he had

Thursday night or this morning. Obviously, she didn't come to work in pajamas, so he'd never seen her sleep-tousled. The sudden attraction wasn't so much of a mystery when he put all of those little things together.

But.

He liked her. He loved the way her eyes narrowed suspiciously each time he suggested more with the Christmas lights just as much as he loved her laugh. Especially the little sarcastic snorts. He liked that she knew who Johnny Mathis was, but the idea of driving around and looking at Christmas lights for fun baffled her. He liked that she ate her cereal dry and seemed to think the story about Oscar was a fib.

No, he wasn't the kind of guy to use women and dispose of them. He wasn't much into hookups, though admittedly, some of his relationships were as short-lived as the life of a shaver. Some didn't even last that long, really.

He winced now at the thought. His parents were happily married; they'd recently celebrated their thirty-somethingth anniversary. His dad sort of adored his mom, and his mom treated his dad like a king. They still hugged and kissed a lot; Dad couldn't seem to keep his hands off his mom. It used to embarrass Scott, but these days, he kind of thought it was sweet.

Which is why he'd never been the hookup for fun kind of guy. But he'd never been a love at first sight guy, either.

"Not first sight, Scott," he reminded himself as he turned back to the ladder. As if to remind himself he was a guy—good grief, thinking about this stuff might lose him his man card if anyone found out—he gripped the sides of the ladder to adjust it just as Nic returned with the clips for the lights.

"What?" she asked.

Distracted by worries over why he was obsessing over her and wondering if he'd gone crazy, he turned to her and almost repeated himself. When their eyes met, however, he closed his mouth without a word. He simply shook his head and then took a box of the clips from her.

"Can I just say something?" She tipped her head as he yanked his gloves off to open the box.

"What?" He blinked at her, worried now that she might spill something he wasn't sure he was ready to hear.

"I don't like pepperoni," she held up a hand and continued, "and maybe we should have picked up a wreath."

He could deal with pepperoni, but Nic's words about a wreath rendered him speechless. She stared at him wide-eyed, waiting for him to respond, but he turned his attention back to the box and grabbed a handful of clips.

"You don't like wreaths?" She cocked a hip and narrowed her eyes at him.

"I do." He nodded. "And it's a good idea. Guess that means we'll be going shopping again."

ELEVEN

THEY WERE OF DIFFERING OPINIONS WHEN THEY FINALLY quit for the day. Nic thought the house looked good; Scott had put up the lights on the straight line of the roof. She had even admitted that the clips had been worth a second shopping trip. The lights were straight and well-spaced, just as Scott had promised they would be. No sags or gaps she spotted so often if she happened to be paying attention to houses and decorations as she drove home in the evenings. Which was next to never.

Scott thought the day's efforts were good, but he still hadn't done the peak of the roof or the dormer windows. He would need an extension ladder for those, and Nic didn't have one. She'd suggested not worrying about it, and Scott had looked at her as if she had suggested they kidnap Santa for the rest of the year. Rather than argue about it, he assured her he had access to an extension ladder, and they could do that tomorrow. When they picked out a wreath for her door.

Somehow, she'd managed to suppress the sigh. More

shopping. For more Christmas things. What in the world had possessed her to say that about the wreath, she would never know. True, her mom used to hang a pretty wreath on their front door. There was a big silver bow at the bottom, a glittery silver reindeer on the side of it. Up close, it was gaudy, and you could see a spot of dried hot glue on the reindeer's hoof, but Nic had liked it okay.

She wondered as Scott climbed down from the ladder the last time if he would be tired and decide to skip the pizza. She wasn't sure what she thought about that. If she wanted to go somewhere with him or not. Her stomach growled, reminding her she was hungry. And pizza sounded perfect.

But did she want to go somewhere with Scott? It wasn't like a date. But still. It was more time spent one on one with him, and what if someone saw them together? It wasn't like they were cops, partners, and a relationship between them wasn't off-limits due to the whole *trust* and *got your back* issues. In fact, Nic wasn't sure there was any policy against dating coworkers at the station—

"Slow it down, Nic," she mumbled as Scott gripped the ladder and picked it up.

"What?"

"Nothing." She shook her head and stepped back so he could make his way to the garage to put the ladder away. He slipped by her without a second glance.

Good grief. Relationship? They'd spent a few hours together decorating her house for a Christmas light contest sponsored by the TV station they both worked for. Hailey had suggested he help Nic, and even if he did like her, that didn't translate to any sort of relationship, anyway. Nothing other than friendship, anyway, and what was wrong with friends grabbing a pizza together?

Because they weren't technically finished with the decorating, Nic couldn't just throw things back in the tub and stick it in the corner until the holidays were over. Instead, she placed extension cords and the new plastic pieces to wrap the new lights around carefully back into the tub, all under Scott's direction. Once they were finished, he followed her into the house and tugged off the black stocking cap he'd pulled out and covered his ears with at some point.

Nic watched him scrub his right hand over his head to smooth his hair down. He balled the stocking cap up in his left hand and eyed her silently. She waited for him to back out of grabbing pizza with her. But he didn't say anything.

Thirsty, she stepped around him to get a glass from the cabinet.

"Do you want something to drink?"

"Please." He nodded.

Behind her, she sensed him moving. Heard him unzip his coat. The same coat rustled a bit with movement. She wondered if he was taking it off; she'd already shed hers and tossed it over the back of the chair he'd sat in this morning. She filled two glasses with ice water, laughing to herself. She probably should have offered to make coffee again. She was cold, but now that she was inside, she didn't feel bad. Scott had been on the ladder, though, and exposed to more of the wind. He might be chilled to the bone.

He was leaning on the counter when she turned to hand him the glass. Coat on but hanging open now. He grinned; his cheeks were ruddy and red from the outdoors. Still, he thanked her for the water and gulped down half the glass in his first swallow.

She sipped hers slowly, eyes pinballing off everything, because suddenly, it felt too intimate to stand here in the kitchen and look at him.

"I could make coffee," she offered now.

He shook his head and lifted a hand to squeeze the back of his neck.

"Nah." He laughed softly. "I'm okay. Kind of warm, actually."

She nodded.

"Granddad and I've been out when it's much colder," he assured her. "And let me tell you, Grandma was a slave driver. She knew just what she wanted us to do, and we weren't finished until the house looked just exactly as she imagined it."

Nic wished for a moment that she could see it, his grandparents' house lit up for the holidays.

"Did you change it every year?"

"Not every year." He pursed his lips in thought. "But often enough."

"And you still do it?"

"Yeah. But not quite like we used to." He met her eyes briefly and offered her a one-shouldered shrug. "Granddad can't get up on a ladder like he used to. He gets around pretty well, but I mean, he's almost eighty. Not a good idea. I have some cousins that help now. Emily's husband if he's around."

Nic nodded. "Sounds nice."

"Do your parents live here?" His question was so unexpected, Nic stared silently for a moment before realizing she needed to answer him.

"Close." She shook her head. "I'm from Lohman. About twenty minutes east."

They held the eye contact for a moment, and then Scott straightened and turned to put his glass in the sink.

"So. Still on for pizza?" He looked at her hopefully. Because she really was hungry, and because she really did want to spend more time with him, she nodded. She wondered if it was too much to ask for time to shower and change her clothes. She hadn't earlier, since he'd been here waiting for her to dress so they could work on the house. "Do you mind if I run home and shower first?"

"Not at all," she answered immediately. "I could use a shower to thaw out."

He pinged her with that grin again.

"Perfect."

"Do you want to meet there?" She stepped up beside him to set her own glass down. Scott turned sideways at the counter. Nic's belly fluttered with nerves when she lifted her gaze to meet his eyes.

"No." He shook his head. "I'll pick you up."

She swallowed hard, ready to protest. But the look on his face stopped her. She wasn't brave enough to define it, but there was something happening. Between them. She wasn't ready to dive in head first. She'd stick with the tried and true tiptoe-in-on-the-shallow-end, but that was better than sitting on the sidelines and watching everyone else, right?

She gasped when he moved to cup the back of her head and leaned in to brush his lips over hers.

"Do you still love him?" Spoken in a gruff whisper, his

words were at odds with the feel of his lips on hers, his face close enough to hers, still, to feel his warm breath on her skin.

Eyes closed, she was surprised to feel his coat under her hand. When had she moved? When had she lifted her hand to rest on his chest?

She shook her head and returned in a nearly breathless whisper, "No."

He kissed her again, but this time he lingered longer, and when Nic parted her lips to breathe, to tug his lip gently with her teeth, he feathered his fingers up through the back of her hair.

The soft, slow slide of his tongue over the inside of her upper lip sent a zap of heat through her. She flexed the fingers on his chest and lifted her other hand to skim those fingers over his cheek. She thrilled to the feel of the rough whisker stubble on his cheek and chin and moaned appreciatively when he flicked his tongue over hers.

"Scott."

Had she said his name out loud? In her head, it was a plea. For more. For another kiss. For his hands on her skin. Had he heard it that way?

His hands remained where they were—one in her hair and the other holding her chin up for his kiss—but he curled his tongue around hers and then plunged deeper.

"I should go." He broke the kiss, but he lingered there in front of her. Nic opened her eyes and nodded. But she didn't drop her hands or step away. Instead, she kissed him, and her heart hit the floor at her feet when she realized that one was on her. She swallowed hard when she saw from the look on his face that he'd noticed it, too. Just a soft, chaste kiss, but it had been her to lean in that time and touch him.

"I'll be back in an hour."

"Okay."

He held the eye contact a moment longer, and then he leaned in again to kiss her cheek. Nic lowered her hands to her sides, her belly flipping again when he gave her another peck on her lips before he backed up and turned away. She watched him pull the back door open and answered him when he called that he'd see her soon.

When he was gone, when she was alone in the kitchen, she stood for a moment, lost in the kiss. No mistaking it now. He might like her as a friend, but there was definitely more to it. And she'd certainly given him the green light.

She noticed his stocking cap on the counter and picked it up. She carried it to her bedroom with her, pressing it to her nose to smell his shampoo and the cold weather and the sun in his hair. She tossed it on her bed and headed for the shower.

Pete hadn't mattered that much, and she didn't feel guilty for thinking that. Because she hadn't mattered that much to Pete. Which was exactly why they'd broken up, and why they were still lukewarm friends. The last time anything had mattered, Callie had lived in her back pocket. Now Callie was otherwise preoccupied a few hundred miles away.

TWELVE

He had purposely suggested grabbing pizza to make it sound casual. For her. But this felt like a date. Rather than finishing the lights and jumping in the truck and running to Pizza King a few blocks from Nic's house, they'd made plans for him to pick her up to go out, after they each took some time to themselves.

And then there was the kiss.

Well, there was some kissing, more than one kiss. Including the one that she'd initiated. True, it had been simple and sweet, but sometimes those kisses said just as much as the long, lingering, intimate kisses. Especially when they were part of a longer, intimate kissing session. Which they'd definitely had in her kitchen.

Scott looked his fill at her while she studied the menu, as if she'd never had pizza before, at the very least like she hadn't had Pizza King before. As far as he knew, anyone who lived in Cloquet had consumed vast amounts of Pizza King. Still, if she was going to use the menu as a way to avoid eye contact, he was going to use the moment as an opportunity to memorize the artful touch of color she'd applied to her eyelids. Nothing dark; the crème or beige or whatever it was had a hint of sparkle to it, which was probably why he'd noticed it. Her blue eyes were framed in thick, long lashes, but then, her lashes were always thick and long. He'd noticed that earlier during their moment in her kitchen. Eyes closed, lashes on her face, lips soft and wet from his mouth.

He scooched a bit, uncomfortable in his jeans, across the booth from her. She was currently squinting at the menu, like she was having a tough time making a decision. He'd seen that look on her face at the station, when she was eyeballing news stories or ratings or even a stupid meme on someone's phone. She nibbled on her lip, and then swung her gaze up so quickly, he had no time to look away.

Busted.

Well. So what? He'd made his intentions pretty clear earlier, hadn't he? If not his intentions, certainly his interest.

She didn't blast him with an angry stare. Or look away as had been the case since she'd opened the door to him ten minutes ago. Instead, she offered him a smile that lit up the room around them.

"What do you like on your pizza?"

"Anything." He shrugged. "Except green peppers."

"Sausage?"

"Sure."

Nic took a drink of her beer. Scott broke the eye contact long enough to look at her fingers wrapped around the bottle.

"Pineapple?" She arched a perfectly shaped brow, the

corner of her mouth perking up in a grin. Was she testing him? Or did she seriously like pineapple and sausage on her pizza? Weird combination, but he'd try it.

"Really?"

"We don't have to." She set her beer down. "My sister and I used to share sausage and pineapple pizzas. Our parents thought we were crazy."

"Doesn't seem that crazy." He rested his elbow on the table and propped his chin in his hand. He decided he had to keep her talking. He wanted to know more about her life, more about the sister she wasn't close to. Besides, he liked the sound of her voice.

And if they weren't talking, he was just going to sit here and undress her with his eyes and fantasize about her. And if the kissing was just a thing that wasn't going anywhere, it would be weird to walk into work Monday with those sorts of thoughts on his mind.

As if they hadn't been there already Friday morning when he walked into the station bright and early after Thursday night and the first kiss and the coffee thing. The one that was definitely not a date.

"Well, she liked bacon and banana peppers, too," she mumbled.

Okay, definitely not something he had tried, but he would if that's what Nic wanted.

"You didn't?"

"Not so much." She closed her menu and set it aside. Scott watched her, dragged his eyes back over her ringless fingers, and up to her face. She'd put on pale pink lip gloss. The navy sweater she wore complemented her light eyes, and he definitely liked her skinny jeans tucked into those long brown boots.

She was simply beautiful, and what Scott loved most was that she hadn't gone over the top when she had dressed to go out with him. Then again, that might be because she didn't consider this a date.

"Tell me about your sister," he said quietly. Her turn to watch him take a drink. He noticed her eyes follow the brown bottle to his lips and then watch him swallow. Scott held the bottle a beat longer, almost startling her when he finally set it down.

"Not much to tell," she said simply.

Seemed to him there might be a lot to tell, but he wasn't sure it would be a good idea to push for more information.

"She was always…" Nic pressed her lips together and raised her eyebrows. "Scrawny. She got sick easy when she was little. The boys in her class picked on her. She had friends, but I watched out for her."

He nodded.

"I think my mom was always waiting for the other shoe to drop, so to speak." Nic pushed her hair back from her face. "She followed Callie around everywhere. Bandaging ouchies before they ever happened. She was always afraid."

"Afraid of what?" Scott shook his head.

"Just that—" Nic stopped when the waitress approached the table to get their order. Scott ordered a sausage and pineapple pie, minus the other stuff Nic's sister liked, relieved when the girl walked away leaving them alone again.

"Just that what?" he prompted her when she didn't seem inclined to continue.

"She never said it, but I think she worried that she

would get sick." Nic bit her lip. "Like the constant colds and ear infections were going to blow up into leukemia or something."

He flinched and hoped like hell that wasn't the case. He hadn't meant to stir up bad memories.

"And did they?"

"No." Nic flashed him a bright, fake smile. "Callie turned into a beauty queen. Healthy and demanding and now and then, happy."

There it was again. The flash of discontent. Oh, there was no mistaking the sharp edge in her voice. Or her words, even. He didn't think anyone—any woman—would want to be described as demanding, so there was definitely a story about Nic and her younger sister, Callie.

But it was more than that. Nic's eyes told a story, always so bright and expressive when she talked. She raved about political news stories, and he'd heard her enthused by sports wins or even just incredible plays on the field or court. She laughed until she cried sometimes—at work and when the crew was out for a drink together. But when she spoke about Callie, her eyes were either cold or haunted.

Not sure how to respond to that, he was relieved when she opened her mouth again to speak.

"Can we not talk about her?" she asked quietly.

"Of course." He agreed with a quick nod. "What should we talk about?"

"Maybe we should talk about the kiss."

Her words were a jolt of heat that cut right through him. Scott searched her gaze for a clue to where she was going. With the discussion about her sister over, her eyes were warm and intense now.

"Which one?" His voice was gruff. Scott hoped that if she noticed it, she thought it was sexy and not just that his heart had pounded a beat harder and kind of robbed him of his breath. Her eyebrows shot up in disbelief. "Well. There've been a few of them now," he reminded her.

"Scott." She laughed softly and lowered her gaze to the table between them. He loved the sight of her slightly pink cheeks, but he wanted her eyes on his.

"Do you mean the first one? That I lied about? Or do you mean the one when you kissed me?"

"There were more than that," she reminded him.

"Oh, I know." He nodded. "Which would you like to talk about?"

"The first one."

"Okay." He took a deep breath and gave her a slow, deep nod. "Hit me. What about that kiss? Did you like it?"

She opened her mouth to answer him, but his question obviously surprised her. She blinked and stared at him silently, cheeks more than tinged pink now.

"Why did you kiss me?"

"Well, I think after the rest of the kissing that's happened, you can answer that yourself."

She tipped her head and shrugged. Not good enough, he supposed. She needed the words, and he decided he wanted to say them.

"I kissed you because I liked the way the wind had mussed your hair when you were up on the ladder. And I liked the winter on your face. And I've worked with you almost every day for a year, and I've never seen that side of you. I was intrigued."

"You kissed me because you were intrigued?"

"There's beauty in the mystery," he said softly. "That's

what attraction is, isn't it? I mean, I see pretty women every day. I see you every day. And suddenly, there was something else about you that attracted me to you, and I had to kiss you."

"You kissed me because I was pissed off about Christmas lights?"

"I kissed you because you were someone other than Nic Collier, news producer. Outside the studio, the station. Away from the crew. You're sweet. You're real. You're—"

"Sweet? Did you say I'm sweet?"

"You're tough, but fair, Nic," he said simply. "At work. Yeah, you can be sweet and still be tough and fair. But you were pissed the other night. At Christmas. At Hailey. At your sister. At the Christmas lights. I wanted to know why."

A deep frown creased her forehead as she reached for her beer again.

"Wow." She swallowed a mouthful and studied him for a moment. "Okay."

"And because I'd been standing beneath you up on a ladder for hours," he admitted. "Your ass looks smokin' hot in the jeans you had on that night."

She snorted so loud, she clapped her hand over her mouth.

"Good to know." She finally got control of herself and met his eyes with a firm nod.

"Well, I hope you don't intend to put those jeans on and climb a ladder just to show it off to someone else."

"No, I don't plan to do that," she assured him with a small smile. "So, to be clear, you kissed me because you're attracted to me?"

"If that's not clear by now, I'm gonna have to assume I don't know what I'm doing with a woman."

"Then why did you lie?" Her voice dropped to a thick whisper now.

"Because I was afraid you were going to deck me."

"I do have a pretty good punch."

"I don't doubt that for a minute."

She raked her teeth over her lip as she considered him for another moment.

"This just feels so out of the blue."

"Why?'

"Well, I mean. You and me? This? Really? We're like sort of friends. Distant work friends. You don't even sit by me at Gin & Harry's when we go out. We've never even shot a game of pool together."

"Every relationship starts somewhere."

"Relationship?" she repeated with a wild look in her eyes.

"No?"

"Maybe." She rubbed her fingers over the bridge of her nose and then ducked her head to hide her eyes behind her hand. Scott might have worried, but he noticed the faint blush in her cheeks. She wouldn't blush if she wasn't into him, would she?

Not to mention the kissing. She'd kissed him back. Every time he had kissed her, she kissed him back. And, *she had kissed him* earlier at her house.

"Maybe you should tell me about Pete."

THIRTEEN

HER CHEEKS STILL WARM FROM SCOTT'S SUGGESTION THAT maybe they were starting a relationship—he could be right, because yes, every relationship started somewhere, and maybe this was how they were going to start something—Nic pressed her lips together and dragged her eyes away from him. She watched the hostess seat a family of five and then turned her attention to a young waiter as he carried a tray of drinks past their table.

"We lived together for a while," she said quietly, still not looking at Scott. "I don't think he was the great love of my life. It didn't break my heart when he left."

"Why did he leave?"

Nic glanced at him, met his eyes briefly, and then looked up as their waitress delivered their pizza to their table. She moved her bottle and scooted place settings and the stack of napkins aside to make room for the pizza pan.

"Can I get you anything else?" the young girl asked

them. Scott tipped his bottle and then looked at Nic curiously as the waitress added, "Another round?"

"Nic?"

"Sure." She offered the girl a smile and then reached to serve the pizza as the waitress walked away. "Honestly, I don't know why he moved in to begin with." She reached for Scott's plate as she shoveled up a slice of piping hot sausage and pineapple pizza. "I mean, we were kind of friends. And then we dated a little. And then he moved in."

"Is that your way of saying you don't think this would work? You and me?"

Nic stilled her hands as their eyes met again. Scott reached for the plate, but she held onto it, shocked by his question.

"Not at all."

The words gushed out before she could stop them. That hadn't been what she wanted to say. Not even close. But she wasn't sure she was ready to dive into anything yet, either. She liked him. She would admit that to herself. After the last couple of days, working on her Christmas lights with him, she was almost ready to forgive Hailey for putting her on the spot and challenging her to the contest in the first place. If not for Hailey, for the stupid light contest, Nic wouldn't have had this chance to get to know him.

He was fun, teasing her about the lights and her less than cheerful attitude about them. And she loved learning about his family Christmases. He had been close to his grandparents, and he was obviously close to his sisters. Nic appreciated family, even though she and Callie weren't close anymore. She also appreciated a man who respected the women in his family; in her opinion, that seemed to suggest he respected all women.

She liked kissing him, too. Wouldn't mind revisiting the scene from earlier in her kitchen.

But no, she wasn't ready to lay her heart out on the table.

Had nothing to do with Pete and the way they'd split. Nic had been cautious about men, about love, for several years.

"I just…" She realized she was still holding his plate and finally let go. With a quick shake of her head, she cleared her throat and then slowly lowered her arms to rest on the table again. "No. I didn't mean that."

How could she tell him that her friendship with Pete had been different from the beginning? Even before this, before the physical attraction, the kissing, her friendship with Scott had been different. Fun and easy. She met Pete when she took her car in to have a new battery put in it. They talked some, hit it off, and spent a few weeks as friends before they started dating. She slept with him the first time after they'd been together nearly a month. She'd never felt that flutter of attraction for him in her belly. Not when he looked at her. Not when he kissed her. Being with Pete had been a bit like settling, and she suspected it was the same with Pete and how he felt about her.

She already felt that crazy, live-wire fluttery attraction to Scott.

Since he'd kissed her that first time, she felt it every time she was with him.

"Pete was pretty vocal about things." She stirred again

to serve herself a slice of pizza, but she didn't eat immediately. "He wanted me to be on screen."

"Like, on the news?" Scott tipped his head.

"Yeah. He didn't like that I was writing the news. That I was behind the scenes."

"Well." Scott snagged his bottle and drained it. Nic looked around for the waitress. She had only one more swallow in her bottle before she would need another. Pizza King did a steady business; tonight was no different. "You're beautiful, but you're also very sharp and determined and good at what you do. So, you should write the news. Or….do what you want to do."

Nic felt a wave of warmth climb her neck and her face. She wasn't beautiful; blue-eyed blonde Hailey Gerritsen was beautiful. Her sister Callie was beautiful. Nic was okay with that; she was okay with average looks, because she knew she was smart.

Still, it was a nice compliment, and the fact that Scott said it and seemed sincere made her heart do a flip-flop in her chest.

"I think that was more the problem." She picked up her pizza and nibbled a bite.

"What do you mean?"

"I think my security in my job made—"

"Your success," Scott interrupted her.

She shrugged and then nodded, begrudgingly. "I think it threatened him. I think really, he wants a woman at home in the kitchen. Barefoot and pregnant."

"And aside from the fact that you're not at home, that you have a great job and you like what you do, and you're good at it—" Scott stopped talking and looked up when the waitress appeared out of nowhere and set two bottled beers on their table. She snatched his empty, but Nic waved her off when she glanced at her. "Do you want that?"

"Do I want to be barefoot and pregnant?" she asked with a snort.

"Well, I guess I'm asking if you want kids, but no, I can't imagine you slaving away in the kitchen, barefoot and pregnant with three or four toddlers running around."

Nic laughed softly. "I don't know. When I was younger, I wanted it all. I always knew I wanted to do something, something important. My mom stayed at home with Callie and me, and she smothered us. I mean…" She waved her hand dismissively. "I told you she fretted over Callie. That was, like, her job. Don't get me wrong; Mom's great. But I always wanted more for myself."

"There's nothing wrong with that."

"But yeah, when I was in high school, when I started dating, I assumed I would meet the right guy somewhere. I figured I would get married and have kids."

"Did you ever meet the right guy?"

Nic jerked her head up to meet his eyes. She picked up her napkin and dabbed at her mouth before she answered.

"I thought I did," she mumbled. "Obviously, I was wrong."

"You were in love before Pete."

She shrugged, reluctant to delve that far into her past, into her one big heartache.

"What about you?"

Scott picked up his beer, but he pointed it at her before taking a drink. "You haven't answered me yet."

"I did, too!" she yelped. They laughed, and Nic drained her first bottle and then picked up her pizza again.

"What about now? Do you want kids?"

She took her time answering him. Remembered a time in her life when she thought she was in love. Well, she'd been head over heels, and she thought he had loved her, too. No engagement rings, no wedding planning. No baby names picked out. But yeah, she had loved Adam; she'd daydreamed her share of weddings and babies with him.

"I don't know," she said softly. "I didn't with Pete."

"You didn't want children? Or you didn't want to have Pete's children?"

Nic cleared her throat and squeezed her eyes closed.

"Isn't it the same thing?"

Scott helped himself to another slice of pizza. He folded it and took a bite and then sat back to chew it.

"So." He arched his eyebrows. "I dated a girl in high school. Like, we started going out at the end of freshman year. Broke up when we were sophomores in college."

"Why?" Nic gasped. She fisted her hands on the table, hoping Scott's break up wasn't as gut wrenching as hers had been.

"It was mutual," he said simply. "I loved her. I think she loved me, but we started out so young. We grew up together. Both of us wanted to try new things. Meet new people."

"Do you still talk to her?"

"Yeah." He nodded and shrugged. "Tori got married three years ago. They live in Colorado. She's a ski instructor. Pretty sure that wouldn't have been the case if she had stayed around here."

"No, probably not," she agreed.

"I don't know." He leaned forward. "It sucked. I missed her for a long time. But it was the right thing to do. And we are still friends. She's happy. She's really happy, and that's what matters."

"Have you dated since then?"

"Dated, sure." He nodded. "I was in a relationship with someone about a year ago. Maybe eighteen months. Maybe she was like your thing with Pete. I mean, Ari and I weren't friends. We didn't hang out and get to know each other first. I met her through a friend. At a party. I asked her out. I almost asked her to move in with me, but I didn't. She was fun. Very pretty. Sexy."

Nic bit her lip when Scott dragged his eyes over her face.

"Well, I thought she was, but when I look at you, I can't really remember why I thought that."

"Scott," she whispered.

"She wasn't…a gold digger. I mean, what you see is what you get, right? No gold to dig. But she worked. She was in human resources at a big manufacturing company, and she loved her job. She just…complained about every-thing I did. If I sold a shot to a magazine, I should have held out for more money, or I should have tried a better magazine. When we went out with friends, she always had a comment about the tie I was wearing, or she would suggest other shoes—"

"Wait," Nic interrupted him with a grin.

"What?" he asked when she only stared at him.

"Just picturing you wearing a tie." She raised her eyebrows.

"Yeah? What do you think?" He tipped his head curiously.

"I would love to see it," she said simply, "but I like you without a tie."

"Ari wouldn't want to eat pizza. She would want a fancy Italian dinner. She wouldn't want beer. She'd want the best bottle of wine on the menu."

Nic nodded.

"I promise you I am nothing like Ari."

"I know that."

Scott held her gaze for several long moments. Even though she felt like he was reading secrets she'd buried deep in her heart and soul, Nic found it impossible to look away. Pete had never looked at her the way Scott did; then again, no one had looked at her this way, as if she was the only woman in the room.

"So." Her face still a bit warm, Nic cleared her throat and reached for her beer. "What about you? Do you want kids?"

She flicked her gaze away as she waited for him to answer. He would want kids; judging from what she knew about him, he would want a big family. She wasn't sure what she thought about it; it seemed a little crazy to be discussing it on their first date. If it was a date. When he'd tossed out the idea of grabbing pizza, Nic thought it was just a convenient, fast way to grab dinner after a long day. Now, though, after that mini-kissing session in her kitchen and parting ways for a while to shower and change and Scott picking her up? It felt like a date.

"I do."

She would swear that his eyes twinkled when he answered her question.

She had a flash of Scott as a dad. A newborn in his arms. A toddler pulling on his legs. Scott putting the kids to bed and then assembling toys for Santa to deliver before Christmas morning. The images warmed her, and for just a second, she let herself believe she could be a part of that. Nic loved Callie's kids, but after all these years of living alone—Pete didn't count in this scenario—she wasn't sure she had what it took to be a good mom. While she wanted to paint herself into her own thoughts of Scott with children, she couldn't even imagine herself pregnant.

"I knew you were going to say that," she told him. She tipped her lips up in a small smile.

"I would love a house full of kids." He shrugged.

Again, Nic found it hard to look away from his intense gaze. She wondered for a moment what kind of lover he was. Most likely, he was as intense and thorough in the bedroom as he was everywhere else. The thought was a flame that warmed her from head to toe, though the fire caught low in her belly and her girl parts. Unable to maintain eye contact while imagining his body pinning her to her bed and his hands claiming her body as his, Nic blinked and dropped her gaze to study her pizza.

Adam had been her first. She supposed for a nineteen-year-old guy, he was okay in bed. They had bumped and fumbled through sex several times. Nic had liked being with him, though he hadn't ever managed to deliver her to ecstasy. Not many guys had. Adam had tried, and at nineteen, she had loved him for it.

She didn't blame him so much anymore for the way things ended. But it was still a sore spot just the same.

"Where'd you go?" Scott's low voice, a little gruff around the edges, pulled her back to the present.

"Hmm?" She lifted her chin and blinked at him, her heart still several years in the past.

"What are you thinkin' about?" he asked her. When he lifted his hand, she assumed he was reaching for his beer. Instead, he reached over the table and covered her hand with his. "You were sort of undressing me with your eyes, and then you looked like a kid with a broken candy cane."

"I was not!" The laughter that roared out of her shocked her. She clapped her hand over her mouth, but she was still laughing. "I was not looking at you like that."

"You were." He nodded, his face carved in a sincere mask. "I was kind of liking it, but that broken candy cane look." He winced and shook his head. "Didn't like what you were seeing?"

"Ohmygod," she whispered and chuckled. "I'm pretty sure I would like what I was seeing if I was undressing you with my eyes. But I wasn't—"

"Swear?" He tipped his head. "I'm not your employee. We're coworkers, so I'm not gonna be upset if you tell me you were picturing me naked."

"Stop it!" She snorted and pressed her hands to her flaming cheeks. "I was thinking that you would be good with kids."

Rather than answer her, Scott moved his hand, snagged his beer, and took a long swallow.

"Is it a little bit weird to you that we're having this conversation on our first date?"

"Is this our first date?"

"Do you want it to be a date?" he hedged.

Nic sighed and grinned. She might not be ready to lay her cards out on the table, but she didn't see anything wrong with letting him know she was interested.

"Yes."

"Okay, then, do you think it's weird that we're having a conversation about kids on our first date?"

"Maybe."

"Really? You're not going to humor me and then dead-bolt your door so I can't get in tomorrow when we start decorating again?"

"Do we really have to decorate more?" She turned up her nose. "And maybe this conversation isn't so off the wall considering we aren't….kids anymore."

"Intentions up front?" He tipped his head. "Like if you absolutely didn't want a family, if you didn't want kids, you would tell me right up front so we could just be friends?"

If she didn't want her own family, this was the time to tell him. Nic studied his face curiously. He hadn't shaved earlier when he had gone home to shower and change clothes. Fighting a sudden desire to touch the scruff on his face, she folded her hands in her lap and nodded.

"I would tell you that right now."

"And instead of telling me that you're back to complaining about Christmas decorations?"

"I am," she agreed with a smile.

"So, I'm Mr. Christmas in this relationship, and you're gonna be bah-humbug?"

"Unless you can make me change my mind, then yes, that's pretty accurate."

"Challenge accepted, Nic Collier."

FOURTEEN

THE DRIVE HOME WAS COZY; SCOTT'S TRUCK WAS WARM AND toasty, and the local radio station played three Christmas songs in a row. Nic didn't sing along, but she didn't complain or roll her eyes. But Scott's mind was rerunning the pizza date for him, and he was stuck on the play of ever-changing emotions on Nic's face while they talked. Even more so in those instances when they weren't talking, and she was either sizing him up for first date sex or looking a little bit lost.

He wanted to hold her hand, but stretching across the cab of the truck to do so was less than romantic. He wanted to ask her why now and then, in the middle of a conversation, her smile didn't reach her eyes. Why she looked haunted. But he wouldn't push her. They had covered some weird ground on a first date; neither of them had professed undying love for the other, but they had skirted some big issues. Tiptoed in around the big stuff. The stuff that could lead to resentment and disillusionment if they didn't make their intentions clear.

Scott understood what she had said earlier. It might be early to talk about families, to talk about having children. But at their age—they were young, sure, but they weren't kids themselves, anymore—maybe it made sense to broach those subjects now. What if they started dating and ended up seriously involved, only for Scott to find out that Nic was adamantly opposed to having children? It was a big deal for him; he had been honest. He would love a house full of kids one day.

She hadn't balked, though.

In hindsight, the whole conversation sort of had him jazzed up and ready to go shopping for rings and houses. On the other hand, the whole conversation and now his ridiculous brain and heart, sort of terrified him. He liked Nic. He liked her a lot. But that was a long way from being in love with her.

Still. You had to leap to fall, and Scott was poised, toes curled around a ledge of some beginning point, ready to take the plunge. True, they'd only spent a few days together one on one, but it wasn't like they had been complete strangers before Thursday. This wasn't love at first sight.

He almost laughed out loud when he realized he was lining up arguments to defend his feelings for Nic Collier, should his mother or sisters attack him about her. They wouldn't, though. All three of them would love her if they met her.

When he pulled into Nic's short driveway, he turned the truck off, but he would swear his own engine was running and purring loudly. He wanted to walk her to the door. He wanted to stay. To kiss her goodnight.

Well, no, he didn't want a goodnight kiss yet. He

wanted to undress her and make love to her, but something told him she wasn't that kind of woman. She might have looked at him with sheer desire earlier, and she might very well have been thinking about the same things. But something told Scott this was different, and it would be better to meander into a relationship with her rather than rush to the finish line.

She wasn't Ari. He wasn't Pete. Those relationships hadn't worked out, but Nic and Scott had a shot at something real.

Scott opened her door for her and offered her a hand as she climbed down from the cab. To his surprise, she linked her fingers through his as they walked up the drive to the door. He stood behind her as she unlocked it and then stepped inside behind her.

"Thank you," she said softly as she unzipped her coat.

"For what?"

"Dinner," she answered. "And for helping me with the lights."

"We should've driven around a bit to look at lights."

Nic offered him a small smile. "Maybe we could do that for a second date."

Scott raised his eyebrows and reached for her. She stepped closer so he could settle his hands on her waist.

"Yeah? You'll go out with me again?"

"I'd like that."

"And tomorrow we're finishing your lights?"

"Okay." She nodded.

He hated that they would be finished with decorating tomorrow. Hanging out with her was fun; he had enjoyed sparring with her over the lights.

"What're we gonna do when we're done with that?" he

asked her. He frowned, hoping she didn't remind him they worked together, so it wasn't like they wouldn't see each other every day.

"We could probably think of something else to do." She shrugged and pursed her lips.

"Too bad you don't have mistletoe." He sighed.

Nic's soft laughter chased a shiver up his spine.

"Know where we can find some?"

She pressed in closer and raised up on her tiptoes. Scott wasn't a player, but he knew what that meant. She wanted a kiss. Who was he to deny her a goodbye kiss? Her soft, clean scent hit him like a drug, but her lips tasted of the beer they'd had with their dinner. He played at her mouth, gentle and easy, in case she wanted to keep it simple.

When she parted her lips and swept her tongue over his, he sank his fingers hard into her backside and hauled her harder against his body. With too many layers between them, Scott groaned with frustration. He wanted skin, and if he couldn't have skin, he at least wanted her damned coat out of the way. He wanted to hold her, to feel her small frame, her curves against his body.

Mouth still pressed to hers, he skimmed his hands up her sides to her shoulders. A tiny little sound in her throat —sounded like a soft little purr—revved his dick up to a full salute. She shimmied against him as he pushed her coat off her shoulders, and then suddenly, her hands were on his face, cupping his chin and framing his lips. Another kiss, this one deeper, more demanding than curious. Scott molded his hands over her butt again. They came up for air, but after a few quick breaths and no words, Nic connected her lips to his again and made it clear that she wanted to be with him just as badly as he wanted her.

"I should go," he whispered when he finally broke the kiss. Pressed to her, head to toe, he felt her panting against him. Unwilling to walk away, he kissed a trail to her ear and then flicked his tongue over her neck. "I don't want to, Nic, but I should."

"I know."

"I don't want to race through this with you."

She nodded, the top of her head resting against his chin.

"I know."

"Do you?"

"Yes."

"I just wanna do this right."

"I want that, too." She tipped her head back to look at him. "Come early tomorrow." She kissed the corner of his mouth. "I'll fix you breakfast."

"Cold cereal?" He frowned suspiciously. "Should I bring the milk?"

"If you want milk, you might want to bring some. But I can fix other stuff. I've got a few kitchen skills."

Scott looked his fill at her face, her chin tilted up so she could see him. She was grinning now, the kind of grin that made him wonder what sort of kitchen skills she was referring to. Maybe she could whip up omelets and bacon, but maybe she was reminding him of the kissing scene they'd had earlier in her kitchen.

"Goodnight, Nic." He dropped a quick peck on her lips and took a step backwards. He was surprised to find that he wanted both—more kissing, of course, but also a home cooked breakfast with her in her kitchen.

"Goodnight."

He carried her smile with him when he left the warmth of her living room. His own mouth was tipped up in a sloppy grin as he drove home. The night had gone even better than he'd hoped it would. He hated leaving her, but it still felt like the right thing to do. Once at home, he kicked out of his shoes and traded his jeans for flannel lounge pants. He considered opening a beer, but he decided against it. It wasn't likely that having a third would give him a headache, but on the off chance that it might, he didn't need one. Honestly, he felt like a kid on Christmas Eve, just knowing he would get to see Nic in the morning.

Channel surfing wasn't usually his thing, but he couldn't focus on anything. In fact, he kept getting lost in thought about Nic—wondering about her and Pete, about her and her sister, what she did for the holidays—and finding the TV stalled out on weird stuff like sappy romantic Christmas movies. He was laughing about that when his phone rang.

His heart slammed against his rib cage on the hope that it was Nic. And then he reminded himself to relax, they had just seen each other, and they had plans to spend time together tomorrow. He answered the phone—it was his sister's name and number on the screen—with a smile.

"Megan." He aimed the remote at the TV to turn it down a bit. "What's going on?"

"Mom's worried you're not coming to Christmas dinner this year."

"Why wouldn't I come to dinner this year?"

"I don't know. You know how Mom is."

He did know how their Mom was. She always worked

herself into a tizzy before the holidays, worried about everything, worried that something wouldn't get done. They'd had Christmas dinner at the same time, at their parents' house, every year for the past eight, but that didn't stop their mom from needing verbal promises that each of her children would be there. Apparently, she had started worrying even earlier than usual this year.

"Tell Mom I'll be there," he told Megan.

"You tell Mom you'll be there. She said you haven't called her in ages."

"I was over there Tuesday, Meg." Scott rolled his eyes. "I helped Dad get all the Christmas stuff out for decorating."

"Oh. Okay."

Scott listened while his sister tried to smother a yawn.

"What'd you do today? You must be getting old if you're tired before ten o'clock."

"I washed windows and cleaned the house."

"Why would you wash the windows in December? Isn't that a spring-cleaning thing?"

"Maybe, but I decided mine needed it. I'm decorating tomorrow. Come over and help me, and I'll feed you as payment."

Her words kind of pummeled him in the gut. He did usually help her with that stuff, but he would rather be with Nic. The trouble with that was that he wasn't ready to say much about Nic and he doubted Nic was ready for him to share much about her with his family.

"I can't," he said, guilt making his chest hurt. "I'm helping a friend decorate. For the station challenge."

"Oh. Cool." She sounded sincere, not like she was pretending to be okay but would tell their mom later that Scott had skipped out on helping her get her place ready for Christmas. "I'll see you later, but call Mom. Please?"

"I will."

"But not tonight."

Scott looked around the room, frown in place, and wondered what time it was. Shocked to realize he didn't have a clock in the living room—he'd only lived there for how long now?—he settled back in the recliner and rested his head on the chair.

"Why not tonight? It's not late."

"It's Saturday night," Megan told him.

"Yep, it is. What's that got to do with anything?"

"It's Mom and Dad's date night."

"And?" He shrugged before he remembered Megan couldn't see him. "Did they go to a movie?"

"No, Scott. They go to dinner and then go home to an empty house. It's their night for sex."

"Eww! Gross, Megan, why did you have to go there?"

"Because you were being dumb." Her soft laughter carried over the phone, making Scott laugh, too, despite the mental image Megan had just delivered to him.

"Don't you think they're done by now?" His question drew a shudder up his spine. Did he really just ask that? First of all, he didn't want to ponder the answer, and second, he didn't want to prolong the conversation.

"I don't know what kind of stamina the men in the family have," Megan answered sweetly, but she ruined the tone when he groaned out loud and she snorted in response. "Call her tomorrow."

"Goodnight, Megan."

"And Scott?"

"Hmm?" He had almost ended the call, but when he heard her call out to him, he put the phone back to his ear.

"Nic, right?"

"I'm sorry?"

"Your friend? From the station? Nic?"

"How do you know that?" He sat forward in the recliner and closed the footrest as if he might have to jump to his feet and defend Nic's honor.

"Well, because I watch the news, and I saw the anchor-woman challenge Nic the producer to do the light contest."

"Mmm. Yeah. I'm helping Nic. Almost done. It's not like…Nic can win, as the station rep in the contest. But it's good for everyone involved."

"Mm-hmm, I'm sure." Megan rushed to agree, making Scott suspicious and protective again. "Are you putting up mistletoe?"

"Come again?" Scott coughed.

"She's super cute."

"How do you know her?"

"I don't, but I saw her on the news."

"I call bullsh—"

"Nicole Collier?" Nic's name sounded pretty good coming from his sister's mouth. Scott wanted to hear all of his family say her name. In conjunction with his. But he bit his tongue. They'd talked about some serious stuff tonight, but he still felt like he needed to approach the whole idea of a relationship cautiously.

"Yeah. I'm helping Nic with her decorations."

"And I'm telling you to get some mistletoe."

Scott sighed. He lifted his free hand and rubbed his eyes.

"What if I told you I don't need mistletoe?"

Megan giggled. "Oooh. My brother thinks he's got game."

"I didn't say I've got game, Meg." He rolled his eyes. "I'm not eighteen."

"And yet, you sound pretty confident."

"Goodnight, Megan."

"Get the mistletoe anyway."

"Why?"

"Because that would be sweet. Romantic."

"Romantic would be taking her flowers. Not hanging mistletoe."

"I'm just sayin'." Megan sounded exasperated. "Goodnight, Scott."

FIFTEEN

Nɪᴄ's ɴᴇᴄᴋ ᴡᴀs ᴄʀᴀᴍᴘᴇᴅ ꜰʀᴏᴍ ʜᴏʟᴅɪɴɢ ʜᴇʀ ᴘʜᴏɴᴇ ᴛᴏ her ear with her shoulder. Her mother had been talking for seven minutes straight. Nic wondered if her mom was breathing, because as far as she could tell, she hadn't paused for a breath once. She flipped the omelet in the skillet and glanced at the clock on the microwave. She hadn't given Scott a time to be here for breakfast, because maybe it sounded a little bit whimsical to just invite him over. Now, with breakfast almost ready to serve, Nic decided whimsy was great for romance novels but maybe not for real life. What if he came over after ten? The omelet that currently looked delicious with cheese and peppers and mushrooms oozing out the sides would be cold and rubbery within ten minutes. The bacon would be cold, and cold grease was disgusting. Sure, they could microwave it, but that wouldn't save the omelet.

"Are you listening to me?"

Nic stood up straight and squared her shoulders. "Of

course, I'm listening to you. Callie's packing for a trip to sunny southern California, and you're going to babysit."

"I would love to travel for Christmas."

No, you wouldn't, Nic wanted to say. Because her mom was a homebody, through and through, most especially at Christmas. But since Callie was traveling this year, her mom had suddenly decided she would like to see other places decorated for the holidays.

"Then why don't you?" Nic asked instead.

"Well, I have to babysit, for one thing."

"Yeah, okay, but Callie's only going to be gone for four days. You and Dad could take off after that. When she gets back."

"Where would we go?" Her mom sounded shocked that Nic would even suggest it.

"Anywhere you wanted, I guess," Nic answered. She flipped the omelet again and rolled her eyes, since her mom wasn't here to see her. She jumped when she heard the doorbell.

"We couldn't possibly go somewhere now, Nicole." This time her mom sounded disgusted with her. "Everything will already be booked this time of year. Did I hear a doorbell?"

"You did," Nic answered. She moved the skillet from the burner, set the spatula down, and went to let Scott in. His smile went straight to her heart, which was nice, since she was talking to her mom about Callie. Again. She raised her eyebrows and mouthed *I'm sorry* as he stepped inside.

He shook his head as he unzipped his coat. Nic watched him slip out of the dark wool to reveal a navy-blue crew neck sweater. When he leaned over to tug his boots off, she drank in the rest of him greedily, taking a moment to study the way his worn jeans fit his thighs.

"Who would be at your house at this time on a Sunday?"

"A friend." Nic kept her answer purposely vague. "We're having breakfast."

"Why didn't she just meet you at the restaurant? It's rude to show up at someone's house on a Sunday morning."

"I invited him here for breakfast, Mom." Nic pinched the bridge of her nose and closed her eyes.

"Him?"

Nic groaned inwardly when she realized her mistake. She should never have let her mom know there was a man here. First would come the third degree about letting him into the house. Second, her mom would ask her a million questions about Scott: how did she know him, were they just friends? Was he good-looking? Why wouldn't she date him? And then, she'd throw in the reminder that Nic wasn't getting any younger.

"I'll talk to you later." Nic spoke firmly, so as to hold off the questions.

"But, who is he, Nic? You never talk—"

"Gotta go, Mom. Breakfast is ready to serve."

When she opened her eyes, Scott was watching her cautiously. She ended the call and sighed dramatically.

"My mother." She offered Scott a smile and a shrug. "Don't be surprised if my phone rings again."

"She'll call back?" Scott jammed his hands in his hip pockets.

"No, my sister will call any minute."

He opened his mouth, and because Nic figured he was

going to ask about Callie again, she nodded her head toward the kitchen. "Perfect timing. Everything's ready."

"Yeah? You just poured the cereal?"

She laughed softly, but her breath caught in her throat when he reached for her hand and linked his fingers with hers.

"But you didn't put milk on it, so there's time for this."

Nic barely had time to register that he was moving closer before he kissed her. Funny, the way her heart could hammer so hard and erratically when the kiss was just a soft, sweet brush of his lips over hers.

"No milk," she admitted. He pressed his mouth to her smile. "But the food's hot."

"So are you."

Her laugh was instant and sharp, and the warmth his kisses had created flooded up over her neck to her cheeks.

"Too much?"

"No." She shook her head slightly.

"Breakfast first." He nodded, but they stood a moment longer and kissed hello.

When they broke apart, she led him to the kitchen.

"Wow. Nic, I didn't expect this." He looked at the skillet and the plate of bacon and back at her.

"I know." She grinned. "You expected dry cereal."

"You didn't have to go to this trouble for me."

"No trouble," she answered simply.

"Can I do anything?"

"You could take the biscuits from the oven."

"Biscuits?"

"They're not made from scratch," she warned him.

"Still." He raised his eyebrows and reached for the oven mitt on the counter. Nic plated their breakfasts.

When Scott set the cookie sheet on the hot pads she'd already arranged on the table and then went back for the coffee, Nic felt another wave of warmth hit her. Only this one was slow and sweet, and rather than rush her cheeks, it flowed through her arms and legs and centered in her belly. It made her a little bit too happy that Scott appeared to be comfortable in her kitchen.

"How'd you sleep?" she asked him when they were both sitting.

"Like the dead, actually," he answered. "I got a solid five hours."

"You're not even being sarcastic, are you?"

"No."

Nic watched him butter a biscuit.

"I did some online shopping when you left." She took a sip of her coffee.

"Really?" He tipped his head. "But not for Christmas lights, right?"

She snorted. "Can I do that? Online?"

"You can get groceries online."

"Now you tell me," she teased.

"But if you had ordered your lights online, we wouldn't have had those fun shopping sprees."

Their eyes met, and Nic felt the flutter of attraction again. More than that, though she couldn't name it. Not yet.

"True."

He took a big bite of his biscuit and groaned appreciatively.

"Will you marry me?"

Nic snorted again and rolled her eyes. "They're not hard to make."

"And yet, I never take the time to pop a can open."

She laughed softly.

"Has your sister called yet?"

Nic had put her phone screen down on the counter, so she had no idea if Callie had called or if her mom might have called back to begin the inquisition.

"No idea," she answered with a shrug.

"Are you ever gonna tell me why you look sad when you talk about her?"

His question surprised her; his tone made her feel safe.

"I don't know," she mumbled. "It's not a big deal. I just…don't like to talk about it."

"Fair enough." He sighed. They ate in silence for a while, but eventually, Scott stirred from his thoughts. "You need some Christmas music."

"You're turning me into a real Christmas elf, Scott." She shook her head. "Like this place is part of the North Pole or something."

"My sister called last night," he told her. "Megan."

"Yeah?" Nic nibbled on a piece of bacon. "Everything okay?"

"She suggested I bring mistletoe here today."

"Did you tell her you didn't need it?"

His grin hit her right in the heart.

"I might have said something like that."

"So, now your sister thinks we're…what?"

"Kissing." He lifted one shoulder and winked at her. "I didn't tell her anything. Just that we're decorating your house as part of the contest."

"Did you tell her you faked mistletoe for the first kiss?"

"Of course not," he scoffed. "A guy's gotta have some pride."

"That or balls."

"Nic!" He sputtered and coughed as he laughed.

"I mean, you kissed me out of the blue." She eyed him thoughtfully. "Definite points for that."

"Well, that's something." His relieved sigh made her laugh.

"But you made up the mistletoe thing."

"Points deducted, right?"

She winced.

"The other kisses, though? I mean, if you're giving points, did they rate me anything?"

"They did," she said quietly.

Scott polished off his omelet and then wiped his mouth with a napkin.

"So. Does your mom think I was here overnight? And that's why you fixed breakfast?"

"No. She heard the doorbell."

"Good."

"I'm not afraid of my mom, Scott," she promised him. "I'm an adult, and I lived with Pete."

"Thank you," he told her. "For breakfast."

"I couldn't have you going back to work tomorrow thinking I only eat dry cereal."

He pushed his chair back with a smile and reached for her. "I'm a little disappointed, though."

"Come back next weekend for cereal." She moved with his gentle tug and settled carefully over him, her thighs straddling his lap.

"You look beautiful." He cupped her chin in his hand and stroked his thumb over her face. Nic raked her teeth over her lip, glad she'd taken the time to do her hair and brushed on blush and mascara. "But I have to admit I liked the pajamas yesterday."

"You're such a guy." She met his eyes.

"I am." He nodded. "I can't get that image out of my head." Nic licked her lips but said nothing. "Is that okay with you?"

"I suppose so." She tipped her head. "But I do have more interesting sleepwear."

"And I hope to see it someday." His enthusiastic laughter made her tip her head back in mock exasperation. But she liked this. Flirting a bit. She felt a little bit sexy at the moment, and it had been a long time since she felt sexy. "But I have zero complaints about yesterday morning."

"Scott."

He kissed her again with that same gentle touch. But Nic leaned closer and pressed into him for more. She and Pete had made out in the kitchen on several occasions, and as frustrated as she was with his sexist comments, she would admit that they had fun sometimes. But this was different. Kissing Scott, wondering what came next with him, wondering about his shoulders and his chest and his waist, was like being nineteen again, doing things with her first boyfriend, doing things for the first time. Kissing Adam had been fun; she'd felt a lot of fluttery stuff with him. But something told her Scott knew exactly what to do with a woman's body to make her weep with joy.

Being a nineteen-year-old virgin in the basement of her boyfriend's house, wanting to do it because she was aroused and curious how it all worked was worlds away from almost thirty, with a few mediocre lovers in her past, and aroused and curious about making love with Scott Woodrow.

As if he could read her mind, Scott angled his head a bit to deepen the kiss. He was still careful, but Nic met him with a greedy tongue and welcomed him. She was aware, suddenly, of their heavy breathing when she felt his warm fingers under her shirt, sliding over her back.

The buzzing of her phone vibrating on the counter across the room was a distraction. But knowing it was Callie calling was the equivalent of having a bucket of cold water dumped over their heads.

"Your sister?"

"I'd bet everything I own that it's Callie." She nodded.

"Do you want to answer it?"

"Nope."

They watched each other as the phone continued to vibrate. When it finally stopped, Scott slipped his hand from her shirt and patted her back. He kissed her again, this time a chaste kiss.

"Maybe we should clean up and knock the rest of the decorating out."

SIXTEEN

THEY BOUGHT A WREATH. SCOTT LIKED WHAT NIC PICKED out, but he was careful not to gush about it too much. For one thing, he didn't particularly want his man card revoked. For another, even though they were sinking into something a little bit sweet and a little bit sexy and so very comfortable, Scott recognized that Nic could still be prickly about the holiday stuff. Scott made sure to grab enough lights and hooks for the dormer windows, and to his surprise, when he was done, he found Nic looking at the yard displays. She didn't buy anything, but he liked that she had stopped to look.

They held hands on the way out of the store. If she hadn't fixed a big breakfast, he would have suggested stopping to grab coffee again. As it was, he decided they should probably get back to her place and get to work on the lights so they could finish the project tonight. The contest deadline loomed, and besides, they were dating now. Or together. Or whatever you wanted to call it. It wasn't like he needed an excuse to be here now, as much fun as working together on her holiday decorations had been.

It took them another couple of hours to get everything done just right and put the remainder of her Christmas stuff away. Once they were finished, they went inside to warm up. He almost suggested they put up a tree—surely, she did a tree—but he was tired, and she turned on football, so they snuggled close on the couch for the late afternoon game.

There was more kissing. As much as he wanted more, Scott didn't mind the kissing at all. When it was dark outside and his thoughts turned to fun, sexy things adults did when it was dark, he climbed to his feet and reached for his coat.

"You're leaving?" she asked from the couch. He was a little bit too pleased that she looked bummed that he might be going home.

"I thought since it was dark outside that we could go on our second date."

Nic looked toward the window, though her curtains were pulled, and then she turned back to him.

"You wanna go look at Christmas lights?"

"I do." He offered her a hand, secretly thrilled when she placed hers in it and let him help her up. "You haven't said. Will you see your family on Christmas?"

"Yeah." She nodded. "We do Christmas brunch at my parents' house. Callie and her family will come into town the day after and stay a few days."

"So, it's just you and your parents for brunch?"

Nic turned off lights, grabbed her coat and phone, and

then stuck her keys in her pocket as they made their way to the door.

"No. My dad's brother will be there. And his aunt. She turned ninety last year. And sometimes they have a neighbor over, so she won't be alone."

"That's nice."

"It is," she agreed. They walked to his truck without words. Scott noticed Nic shiver as she climbed up into the passenger seat. "They're good people, Scott. Don't read me wrong about that."

"They must be," he said simply. "Because I would say the same about you. Even before you kissed me."

She aimed a grin at him as she buckled her seatbelt. Scott moseyed around the front of the truck to his side. The air felt colder than it had earlier in the day, making him glad they finished the lights early. He eyed the darkening sky as he settled into his seat and buckled up. He loved white Christmases, but it was much too early to wish for holiday snow.

"Do you still do gifts? I mean, do your parents give you gifts?"

"Little things," she answered with a nod. "Books. Gift cards for movies."

"Fun stuff."

"Yeah. Mom used to buy me clothes, but we don't have the same fashion sense, so she gave up trying."

Scott started the truck, but he studied Nic's face for a moment. She stared out the windshield, seemingly unaware of his attention.

"There you go again, looking all sad." He reached across the cab of the truck to nudge her. "You okay?"

"Yeah. I was just thinking. Mom and I are totally opposite. In pretty much everything. I used to think I was adopted."

"Every kid thinks that," he reminded her. "At some point in childhood, every kid thinks he or she was adopted."

"I know." She grinned. "It just bugged me that Callie was like a mini-version of my mom." She sighed and shrugged absently. "I guess it still does now and then."

"Is it possible she's more like your mom because your mother was so overprotective of her? Maybe they were together more than you were with your mom?"

"Absolutely possible," she admitted. "Besides, I'm a lot like Dad, so I know I'm at least his kid."

"Do tell."

"He doesn't love Christmas."

"That all?" Scott frowned.

"No. We both love mustard. On sandwiches. In baked beans. As a dipping sauce. We have the same sense of humor. We both like comedies. We're interested in history. Dad and I would sit and watch biographies or documentaries while Mom and Callie did all the Christmas stuff."

Scott pursed his lips and shrugged. "Nothing wrong with that."

"The only thing I get from Mom is my smile," she told him.

"Well, then, Nic Collier, I like your mom's smile."

He eased the truck into gear, and they were off. Christmas songs played now and then, but they were peppered with regular present-day country music songs.

Nic didn't seem to mind either. Traffic was light, and he drove through neighborhoods rather than the main city streets in Cloquet.

"You know what would add to it? Make it prettier?"

The truck idled at the curb as they both leaned forward to appreciate several houses in a row, all lit up for Christmas.

"What?" She tilted her head and watched him expectantly.

"Snow."

"Yeah, I'm just not sure this is gonna work out."

She was grinning, and then she was laughing. Scott rolled his eyes, but he laughed, too.

"Not a fan of snow, either?"

"Are you saying you are?"

"For the holidays," he answered. "Besides, sled riding is fun."

"If you say so."

"When's the last time you played in the snow?"

"Um." She nodded her head from side to side. "Maybe two years ago. With Callie's kids."

"And that wasn't fun?"

"Well, it was, but I told you I'm crazy about her kids."

"You don't think you could have fun in the snow with me?"

Nic studied his face for a few seconds, before offering him a small smile.

"I think you could probably make anything fun," she admitted. "Except maybe dental checkups."

"Well, I mean, I'm not magic." He shrugged.

"What do you do for Christmas?"

"Dinner at my parents' house. My sisters will be there.

Two aunts and uncles. My grandpa. Other family members drop in through the evening, but Mom puts out fresh snacks and goodies for them."

"Fun."

"We play games. Do you?"

"I play games with Callie's kids."

"Callie doesn't play?"

Nic flicked her eyes up to look at him. That flash of pain in hers ripped through him again like scissors.

"Callie and I don't do much together anymore," she said softly.

"Can I ask you something?"

She flinched, and Scott wondered yet again what secrets she had stowed away that involved her sister. He wasn't going to ask anything about her. If she wanted him to know, she would tell him.

"Sure."

"Tomorrow. At work." He drummed his fingertips on the steering wheel. "Are we just coworkers? Friends?"

"Thinking about having your way with me on the news desk?" She arched her eyebrows.

Scott laughed and shook his head. "Maybe. No, but thanks for putting that idea in my big head, because now the little one's not gonna let me sleep at all tonight."

"We keep talking about sex, Scott." She tossed the words out easily. "When are we going to do something about it?"

"Soon." He nodded. "This is only our second date."

"You're a third date sex guy?"

"I'm a it'll-happen-when-it's-supposed-to kind of guy," he answered.

"So, it's going to happen?"

"Well, you should probably sleep with me before you marry me. Just to make sure you approve of the merchandise."

"And this is a proposal based on my ability to pop open a can of biscuits and bake them for nine minutes at four hundred and twenty-five degrees?"

"Mad skills," he mumbled.

"Are you asking my permission to tell people we're dating? Or are you asking if you can play with my butt at work?"

"I wouldn't do that at work," he said sincerely. "You know I have absolute respect for you and all working women."

"So, you just wanna tell people?"

"I just want to know if it has to be a secret."

Nic considered his question for a moment and finally shook her head. "No. I don't think it needs to be a secret."

"Good."

"Just the same, please don't write anything about *for a good breakfast, call Nic* on the stalls in the men's room."

"Damn." He winced. "You got me."

"Scott?"

"Hmm?"

"Are we going out next weekend?"

"We are," he answered firmly, "but please don't tell me you're a weekend only dater."

"No, I'm not." She grinned. Her eyes kind of sparkled, he decided, and they were prettier than any lights outside the truck. He put it back in gear and pulled away from the curb. "But I don't get too wild through the week. That early hour's a killer."

"Got it." He nodded.

"Do you ever see Ari?"

"No." He glanced at Nic. "I haven't seen her in well over a year. Are you worried about Ari?"

"No."

"Because I don't play games, Nic. I'm not that guy."

SEVENTEEN

Nɪᴄ ᴡᴀꜱ ᴜꜱᴇᴅ ᴛᴏ ɢᴇᴛᴛɪɴɢ ᴜᴘ ᴛᴏ ʙᴇ ᴀᴛ ᴡᴏʀᴋ ʙᴇꜰᴏʀᴇ ᴀ ʟᴏᴛ of the world stirred, but she hadn't lied to Scott. She had nothing against going out through the week, but she rarely stayed out late. Her alarm dragged her from a dream about building a snowman with Scott, so she wasn't thrilled about getting up the next morning. On the other hand, she would see him at the station. That thought made her get out of bed. Put a smile on her face, too, though she wanted to be cool enough not to shower and dress with a sloppy grin.

Not that it mattered since she was alone.

When her phone rang on her drive to the station, she tapped the answer button assuming it was Scott. Her sister's booming voice over the car speakers via Bluetooth threatened to steal away her good mood.

"Why are you calling me at this hour on a Monday?" Nic asked with a small sigh of defeat. Callie had always been a thief; she'd stolen more from Nic than she could ever get back—joy, love, contentment, loyalty, just to name a few things.

"Good morning to you, too," Callie said quietly. "I'm calling now because you blew me off yesterday."

"I didn't want to talk to you." Nic kept her right hand on the steering wheel, but with her left, she rubbed the spot between her eyebrows where a Callie headache was already brewing.

"Thanks, Nic."

"I was busy, Callie. And you knew it."

"I called—"

"You called because Mom called you to tell you I had a guy at my place."

"Well." Callie sounded indignant. "It's been forever since you dated anyone. Pete's old news. What's going on?"

"Nothing." Nic rolled her eyes. "Scott and I are friends. We work together."

She held her breath, hoping Callie would let it go and that Scott would forgive her the fib. She had her reasons for not wanting to share more than that with Callie or her mom.

"But are you dating him?"

"Why does it matter to you?" Nic slowed at a stop sign. She eyed the giant gold bells that decorated the city streetlights down Maine Street. Were they new this year, or had she just never taken the time to look at them? Maybe Scott had taught her to slow down and look around, and she had most definitely enjoyed driving around with him last night to look at the Christmas displays in some neighborhoods on the north end of Cloquet. But she wasn't sure she liked the gold bells the city had used to decorate. Maybe she would have to drive down Maine after dark to see if they lit up the street with lights. Maybe Scott would go with her.

"Why—? Because, Nic. You're getting old."

Nic snorted.

"Seriously?" Callie whined. "You deserve someone to make you happy."

"You're totally jumping the gun, Cal." Nic waved and smiled at a woman as she hurried across the street in front of her. Also new. She wasn't a rude person; she'd never been anything but polite and courteous. But she'd never felt inclined to wave at strangers, either.

And Callie totally wasn't jumping the gun, but damned if Nic would tell her that.

"What's he like?"

"He's got two legs and two arms. And a face. And he speaks English."

"Shut up." Callie groaned. "Humor me. Is he hot?"

"Yes, he is," Nic answered. She slowed at the turn to the station parking lot and flipped her signal on.

"Are you sleeping with him?"

"Would he be ringing my doorbell on a Sunday morning if I were sleeping with him?"

"Why aren't you sleeping with him?"

"I've gotta go, Callie." Nic ended the call as she pulled into her space. She sat for a second in the warm car, her mind on Callie, her stomach twisting with guilt. What if Callie had needed to talk to her about something? What if something was wrong? She did call now and then to stick her nose in Nic's business, and it was a pretty good bet that this one was prompted by their mother. But still.

Nic snatched her phone up and texted Callie.

Is everything okay?

She stared at her phone, watched the three floating dots that indicated Callie was answering her.

Callie: No. My sister just snubbed me.

Nic: I didn't snub you.

Callie: You hung up on me.

Nic: I'm at work. I'm busy.

Callie: Just tell me. Do you plan to sleep with him?

Nic: Is Jeff not taking care of your needs, Cal? Is that why you feel the need to be nosy about my sex life?

Callie: When's the last time you had sex, Nic? It might put a smile on your face.

Nic: I gotta go. Kiss the kids for me.

A gust of cold wind greeted her when she climbed from her car. Nic shoved her hair from her face and almost slammed her car door shut. Callie's calls—there weren't many, thankfully—always put her in a mood. Normally, a conversation like she'd just had with her sister would follow her around all day like a dark cloud. Nic aimed her key fob at the car and beeped the locks and then turned to head across the lot to the building.

Not today. She wouldn't let Callie or her mother—since Mom had obviously put Callie up to the call—ruin today. She shoved the phone call out of her mind and thought about the weekend with Scott. Remembering that she'd been frustrated with him and with Hailey last Thursday when he had shown up to help her with the lights, she chuckled at how quickly that had changed. Maybe she should thank Hailey for sending him over. Well, Scott said Hailey had mentioned that Nic was working on lights, that she hadn't directed him to head over to help. But still. Maybe Nic should thank Hailey for the nudge.

Odds were, without it, Scott wouldn't have just shown up, and Nic sure wouldn't have made any moves on him at the station or Gin & Harry's.

Nic found herself humming Christmas carols while she pulled the morning's news together. Wouldn't Scott get a kick out of that? She also found it hard to hold down the smile, though it wasn't as if she normally worked with a scowl on her face. As the station came to life again and everyone filed in for the daily meeting and story assignments, Nic watched for Scott. When she did see him, she could swear electricity crackled between them, even from across the room.

He kept his eyes on her as he poured himself a cup of coffee. Needing to say something to him before the day really got going, something private, she moseyed over to the coffee table to pour her own. She didn't necessarily need it or want it, but she sidled up next to him and breathed deeply. She smelled coffee, sure, but so much better, she smelled Scott's clean, fresh scent. He grinned down at her; Nic would swear his eyes twinkled. It was official. She was either high on Christmas, or she'd plunged headfirst into a serious crush.

"Good morning." His quiet gruff voice chased goosebumps over her arms and legs. Nic's eyes were drawn to his smile. Which made her remember those kisses. The first one that had come out of left field. The one where she'd leaned into him and kissed him, and he'd kissed her back. And the one where he'd pulled her over to straddle his lap. When he'd slipped his hand inside her shirt and touched her back. Definitely past the serious crush stage.

Remembering that kiss in the kitchen, the feel of his fingers on her back, and the way her body had responded reminded her that her sister had called and interrupted them.

"What's wrong?"

She sighed and took the cup he handed her, noticing that he'd added just a touch of cream to it. The same as she had done yesterday at breakfast.

"Just talked to my sister," she said quietly.

"Everything okay?"

"Yep." Nic nodded. "She was just calling to see if we're sleeping together."

Scott choked on a swallow of coffee. He thumped his chest and looked at her with watery eyes.

"Did you tell her not yet?"

Nic grinned and shook her head.

"Are you supposed to report in after we do?"

"Nope."

"You don't kiss and tell?" Scott tipped his head.

"Not to Callie, no."

The ghost of a frown flashed over his face, but it was gone just as quickly as it appeared.

"I would love to kiss you right now."

"I'd have to slug you."

"I know." He winced and shrugged. "Trying to decide if it would be worth it."

"Mean right cross," she reminded him.

"Still." He arched his eyebrows. "Little bit of pain would be worth a taste."

"You should write poetry," she told him, but she had to laugh.

"Have dinner with me tonight?"

"Are you tired of Christmas?"

"No." He looked around the conference room. Nic took a peek over her shoulder to see that it was filling up. Time to get busy.

"I need to put my tree up."

"Do you usually put a tree up?"

"I do." She nodded. "But it would be more fun with your help."

"Got any mistletoe?"

Nic snorted and covered her mouth. Scott eyed her with amusement and nodded as he moved away from her.

"I'd love to help you put your tree up."

To hide her silly grin, she sipped her coffee, surprised to realize her hands were shaking. Only two guys had that effect on her; Danny Pfiffer in third grade—first kiss— and Adam Monahan—when she'd given him her virginity. What did that say about Scott, she wondered, as she took her place at the table to dole out the workload for the day.

She loved her job, and after a few moments of her heart pitter pattering over what was happening with Scott, she settled in and worked her way through the list of assignments. Her cup was empty when the meeting was over, but she didn't want more coffee. She didn't need more coffee; her heart was beating like a hummingbird's wings already.

"Hey." She leaned back in her chair when she realized Hailey Gerritsen was still at the conference table with her.

"Your house looks great," Hailey announced.

It did. Two of Nic's neighbors had given her a thumbs up already, one last night when she and Scott came back from their Christmas lights date, and the other this morning when she backed out of her drive. Mr. Peterson worked the graveyard shift at an all-night convenience store, and he had just been coming home when Nic left.

"Thanks." Nic nodded, choosing not to wonder when exactly Hailey had seen her lights.

"Makes me wish you could win." Hailey smiled wistfully.

"If I did, I'd give the money to the schools anyway."

"Of course, you would." Hailey rubbed her eyes. "I would go on some extravagant vacation. A cruise, maybe."

"I know."

Nic did know, because Hailey was so much like Callie, it was sometimes easy to suspect they were the same person.

"Did Scott help you? With the lights and stuff?"

"Yeah, he did. Thanks for sending him over." Nic stared at Hailey boldly. "The place wouldn't look nearly as good if he hadn't helped me. Well. Let's be honest. I helped him."

Hailey laughed softly and tapped the tabletop as she stood.

"You guys looked pretty cozy this morning."

Nic bit her lip and studied Hailey, wondering what her angle was.

"He's a good guy," she finally answered. "He would have helped anyone with that project."

"True, but he's only been making eyes at you, not anyone else."

Nic tipped her head and frowned.

"I know. You haven't seen it." Hailey shrugged a shoulder. "But he's been watching you for a long time, Nic."

"Are you saying you sent him to help me as a way of setting us up?"

Hailey shrugged dramatically now.

"Maybe."

"Wow." Nic pushed her own chair back to climb to her feet. "I'm not sure how I feel about that."

"You just said he's a good guy. What's wrong with someone giving you both a little nudge?"

Probably nothing. But being that Hailey reminded Nic of Callie, she didn't trust her.

"We put Christmas lights up, Hailey," Nic said simply. "Don't make that a big deal."

Nic hoped for the second time that day that Scott would forgive her for making less of what they might be doing. She figured he would be okay with the fib to Callie, but maybe not Hailey. Not without further explanation, and she wasn't ready to get into any of that.

EIGHTEEN

SCOTT HELPED NIC WITH HER TREE. IT WAS A SMALLISH, artificial tree, and thankfully, the lights worked when she plugged them in to test them, so the decorating went quickly. He would have asked her to help him with his, but his sisters had already done it. Turned out okay, though, because even though there was no more decorating to do, he and Nic spent most evenings together. They were together more than they were apart, which was more than fine with him.

They watched football again on Monday, after topping her tree with a silver star. Scott was delighted to find out she was a Chiefs fan. He liked the Cowboys, but he loved that she was a football girl. They grabbed dinners out, and they saw a couple of movies. And after each excursion, Scott drove through different neighborhoods, and they looked at lights. Now and then, they critiqued color or quantity, but to his surprise, Nic seemed to find the whole thing as relaxing as he did.

Their coworkers figured out that they were sort of

dating, though Hailey told him Nic had said they were just friends. Because Nic had already made comments to him about Hailey that suggested there was friction between them, it didn't bother him that Nic had downplayed their relationship. It did make him more curious about Nic's attitude toward Hailey, but since Nic took the teasing from coworkers about them dating with a smile, he didn't push it.

As someone who always enjoyed the season and loved Christmas, Scott decided spending time with Nic made it more fun. He'd had girlfriends over the holidays before; he had spent a couple of Christmases with Ari. But something about being with Nic felt different; everything felt new to him. Obviously, this wasn't the first Christmas Nic had put up lights and gotten into the holiday spirit—after all, there was the thing about shopping for lights with Pete. But Scott hoped she was feeling something a little bit more this year, just as he was.

"What're you doing?" Nic watched him grope around under the driver's seat in the truck. They'd spent the evening at a local bar, both of them kicked back, sipping wine, and enjoying a festive night out. The bartender, Jimbo—Scott knew him just from hanging out there now and then—wore a Santa hat, one of the waitresses wore a light-up reindeer headband, and the music playing was a fun, Christmas mix. As always, when they left, Scott drove around a bit to look at lights, but he'd cut it short and brought her home early tonight.

He wanted to talk about the office Christmas party, which was only a week away. He also wanted to ask her what her plans were for the holidays. They'd discussed traditions, but Scott wanted to be with her over Christmas, and if it meant missing his mom's family dinner, he was willing to risk his mom's wrath.

"Ah. There we go." He curled his fingers around the hammer he'd brought with him and flashed Nic a smile as he waved it at her.

"Are we building something? Santa's workshop, maybe?" She grinned as she unbuckled her seatbelt. "Or should I be worried? Are you an axe murderer on the side?"

"It's a hammer, not an axe," he corrected her as he backed up and swung his door closed. Nic slid out of her side and closed her door as he rounded the truck to walk with her up the drive.

"So, you're a hammer murderer?" She linked her fingers with his and peered up at him.

"Really? Is that a thing?" He shook his head. "Doesn't have the same catchy ring to it."

"Okay, so, then we are building something?"

"Nope."

At the front door, Nic dug for her keys and jammed one in the doorknob.

"Wanna come in?" she asked with a grin.

"Yep."

Once inside the house, Nic shrugged out of her coat and tossed it on the back of the sofa. Scott set the hammer down on the cushion and took his own coat off. Nic watched curiously as he pulled a sprig of mistletoe from his coat pocket, picked up the hammer, and then studied the doorframes in the room to find the best place to hang it.

"Um." She cleared her throat. "What are you doing?"

"Hanging mistletoe."

"Why?"

"So I can kiss you."

"Why would you suddenly need mistletoe to kiss me?" She folded her arms over her chest, clearly amused.

"My sister said it would be romantic." He shrugged.

"Really?" She pursed her lips and considered him and then the doorframes—the front door, the coat closet, the door to the hallway, and the kitchen door.

"You don't think so?"

"Maybe." She eyed the hallway and then turned back to him.

"Nic?"

"Hmm?"

"I want you to go to the office party with me."

She might balk. It was one thing for their coworkers to know they were dating, but something completely different for Nic and Scott to be seen together in a social setting. Because if they were in a party atmosphere, there was a definite possibility he would be less than professional. He would definitely put his arm around her, and at some point in the night, he would have to kiss her. And if there was music and dancing, he was sure as hell going to hold her tight.

"Yeah?"

He glanced at her, mistletoe and hammer still in his hands. She watched him with wide eyes.

"Is that a yes?"

"You're ready to go public?"

"They all know we're dating," he reminded her, and then he added, "Even Hailey."

She nodded, the bit about Hailey not fazing her a bit.

"Right, but it'll be different when they see us together. You ready for that?"

Scott laughed softly. "I thought I would be asking you that. I'm ready, Nic. I don't care who knows."

She blinked at him and then offered him a small smile and a nod.

"It's a yes," she said softly. "I'd love to go to the party with you."

"And—"

"Don't you need a nail?"

"What?"

"A nail?" She nodded at the hammer in his hands.

"Got one."

"Really? You came prepared, huh?"

"I did. Where should I hang it?"

"Well." Nic cleared her throat and reached for him. "Since you asked."

Scott watched her curl her fingers around his forearm. He followed her, assuming she was heading to the kitchen. Instead, she led him down the hall to what appeared to be her bedroom.

"Are you sure?" He looked up at the doorframe and then at Nic when she stepped inside the room to turn the bedside lamp on.

Nic met his eyes as she turned to him. The heat in her eyes was unmistakable. She was inviting him into her bedroom. She wanted him; she wanted to be with him. The small smile on her lips was powerful and knowing and sexy as hell.

"I'm sure."

Scott watched her take the hammer and the mistletoe both from his hands and set them on her dresser. Her hands were small, but at the moment, they were strong enough to have captured his heart. Blunt, unadorned nails, no rings, Scott decided her hands were beautiful, because they wanted to touch him.

"Where's the nail?" The ornery grin flashed again, and Scott decided he liked it as much as he liked that small sexy smile of a minute ago. "We don't need any injuries."

He tipped his head back and chuckled.

"It's in a plastic bag in my coat pocket."

"Good. Can't imagine trying to explain that to people."

"Nic."

"Hmm?" She pressed her fingertips to his chest and walked them slowly upward to the collar of his shirt.

"C'mere."

Scott wrapped his arms around her and hauled her up against his body. She moved willingly, her arms sliding up over his shoulders and her hands clasping behind his neck. Her lips were soft, but her mouth was hot and hungry against his. Scott smoothed his hands over her butt, moving his mouth to her neck when she turned her head.

"Why would you think you need mistletoe to kiss me?" she asked with a soft laugh.

"I told you Megan said it would be romantic."

"You tell your sister you don't need any help with romance, Scott Woodrow," she answered.

"You're good for my ego."

"I don't want your ego," she whispered as she curled her fingers around his neck. "I want you."

"This is gonna change things, Nic," he reminded her, but his hands were on the tail of her shirt ready to move, to touch, to claim her as his.

"What do you mean?"

"If we make love tonight, there's no way I can act like we're work friends who sorta started dating and we're hanging out for the holidays."

She tipped her head and arched her eyebrows.

"But things don't change at work."

"No." He shook his head and slipped his hand inside her shirt. "But...I can't pretend to all of them that we're just hookin' up, either."

"Okay." She nodded. "Me, too."

Her gruff whisper made his heart beat a little faster.

"You're sure?"

"I'm a little out of practice, Scott, but yes, I'm sure." She stepped back and trailed her fingers down his chest again. "I want to be with you."

He wasn't a kid, and he'd dated a lot of women. Liked them, loved a few of them. Slept with them. Sex had been everything from painfully awkward to sweet to smoking hot and everything in between. But something told him that making love to Nic would be different, a combination of all of that together and still, somehow, more. They hadn't really done awkward, but with that first kiss and his fib about mistletoe, it had been less than smooth.

He undressed her in the lamplight, his hands slow with the need to appreciate every inch of her smooth skin. Her sighs of pleasure bolstered his moves, made his hands both steadier and a bit shaky at the same time. Hungry to touch her, to experience everything with her—now— Scott refused to rush through the first time out of desperation.

In pale blue lace and nothing more, lips sealed with his, Nic stopped his hands before he could take off more.

He stilled his hands, worried that she had changed her mind. But she simply pulled back to offer him that small, sexy smile as she moved her hands to his waist to push his shirt up over his stomach. Her hands were warm and soft on his skin. Scott had been so focused on her, he hadn't realized how badly he needed her touch.

He tugged the collar of his shirt up and over his head, Nic's hands already unbuttoning his jeans.

"Please tell me you have condoms." She eyed his waistline with greed as she parted the denim and pushed it open to reveal his black briefs.

"I have condoms," he answered. "Not because—"

She cut him off with a quick shake of her head. "I don't need to know why you have them, just that you do."

"I have a few." He tugged his wallet from his back pocket.

"A few?" Head still tipped to study his fly, she raised only her eyes to look at him. A grin played at her lips. Scott might have been embarrassed at the way his dick throbbed at the thought of those lips on him, but they were past that now.

"Three."

"Hmm." She quirked an eyebrow at him. "So, maybe your ego will be a good thing for me?"

"That's not ego, Nic," he promised her. "That's me being crazy about you."

Nic took his wallet so he could kick out of his jeans.

"You know what I decided?" he asked as he eased her back to her bed.

"What did you decide?"

"Your eyes are prettier than any Christmas lights."

Her soft laugh was like velvet on his skin.

"And your sister thinks you need help in this department?"

"Well, not sex."

"I don't mean sex."

They fell to the bed together, but Nic quickly moved to straddle him and pin him down.

"I don't think I've ever met anyone like you."

"Well, I hope not." Scott skimmed his fingers up over her back and unhooked the scrap of blue lace that covered her breasts. "But you could expound on that a bit if you wanted to."

She shrugged the lace off and let it drop to the bed before leaning over him again.

"I've never known a man so into the holidays." She smoothed her hand over his forehead.

"I'm not into the holidays, Nic. I'm into you."

"I'm glad." She dropped a kiss on his cheek. "But you are into Christmas. It's very sexy, really."

"I have to touch you." He captured her hands in his and gently flipped her over to her back. "I never thought being into Christmas made a guy sexy."

"I think it's more that you're into family and traditions and—" She gasped out loud when he kissed a trail from her chin to her breast. "I love that about you."

"You love that about me? That being...my mouth... here?" He kissed her other breast as he settled his weight over her.

"Yes."

"While I have you occupied here." He nudged her nipple with the tip of her tongue. "Will you wear a dress? To the party?"

"You want me to wear—" She moaned softly when he

closed his lips around her and suckled her nipple into his mouth.

"A dress."

"Okay."

"And, Nic?"

"Ohmygod, Scott." She laughed and wrapped her arms around his back. "Yes, whatever you're going to ask, yes. Stop torturing me and get naked."

He moved quickly, stripped his own briefs off as he climbed to his feet. Nic lifted her hips when he hooked his fingers in her panties.

"You just agreed to spend Christmas with me," he informed her as he slipped the lace over her feet and tossed it aside.

"Where else would I spend Christmas, Scott?" She reached for him, a mix of the feisty grin and the sexy smile on her face.

NINETEEN

SCOTT WAS JUST THE SORT OF LOVER NIC ALWAYS ASSUMED he would be. Well, if she had given any thought to being intimate with him before he showed up to help her with lights. But really, he was fun and generous with friends; how would he not be the same in the bedroom with a lover? She hadn't been with anyone since Pete, and mostly, she was okay with that. She missed sex, but she hadn't resorted to surfing cable channels or the Internet for porn or even just gratuitous nudity.

But spending so much time with Scott, getting to know him over the past weeks, had shifted something inside her. Kissing him had lit her up inside like the lights he had hung on her house. And acknowledging their attraction to each other, discussing it openly kindled that fire until she was ravenous for him. Maybe he had hoped to end the Friday night date snuggled up to her in her bed, too. Maybe the hammer and the mistletoe had been his good luck charms or something. He most definitely hadn't needed them.

He was considerate in her bed, but he was playful, too, and Nic suspected that once they spent this first night together, once they spent a night making love, he might prove to be a little bit dirty and hardcore, too. As much as she loved the generous side of him, the man who touched her with love and skill and drove her to the brink of orgasm several times before pushing her over the edge and sending her straight to the stars, she couldn't wait to play with that dirty, sexy man, either.

They moved their private party to her living room after two rounds and snuggled together on the sofa and watched a Christmas movie. The lights on the tree cast a magical feel over the room, and Nic loved that glow for the first time since she was a kid living at home. But she knew the magic for her this year was the man whose arms held her close as they lay together. Falling like this was new to her, but she knew the flutter in her belly, in her heart, was the start of something big.

He stayed overnight, and neither of them gave a thought to his truck parked in her drive. Nic didn't particularly care if everyone in their worlds knew they were intimately involved, though she wasn't one to share details with anyone. Once upon a time, Callie had been her closest friend, but times had changed, and Nic wasn't one for girl talk at work. She would be happy, proud, to walk into the office party at Scott's side, but she wouldn't share with Hailey or Elin or Cathy or any other coworker that Scott was a master with his hands or that he kissed her like she was the only woman in the world.

She might introduce him to her parents, but she had no intention of inviting them, or Callie for that matter, into their relationship. When her mom called late the next morning, waking them—they'd gone back to bed after midnight, but they had talked and touched and kissed and made love again before giving in to sleep—Nic ignored the phone. They shared an intimate breakfast, feeding each other grapes and cheese. Scott toasted bread for them, and they laughed at his kitchen expertise. They sipped coffee in the living room by the tree and shared Christmas memories. Nic dug up stories about her and Callie she thought were long forgotten, and she was relieved that she could laugh with Scott, feel good about remembering her childhood with her sister.

After a long weekend of nothing but each other—Scott went home once to shower and pack clothes, and thankfully, grab more condoms—Nic found it hard to go back to work. Waking next to him and spending hours on end with him had been cozy and fun. Didn't matter that she loved her job; the thing with Scott was better. At least they saw each other at work. And they spent evenings together. Except Thursday, when Nic panicked about what to wear to the office party and went shopping to find a dress. She hadn't worn one in ages. He might have coerced her into agreeing to dress up for the party—he might have talked her into bank robbery if he had continued kissing a southern trail over her body while making demands—but the thought of dressing for him, of finding something a little bit sexy, had her all fluttery again. She'd even suffer the torture of sexy shoes to turn him on, not that she would tell him that.

Times like those, though—shopping for girly things— made Nic miss Callie. Made her wish for closer girl-friends. Probably Hailey would have jumped to go with her, but Nic had no intention of inviting Hailey inside her private life. As nice as she could be at the station, Nic associated that sweet, beautiful smile with mean girls. And Callie. Even though her sister hadn't *really* been a mean girl, not when they were younger.

She tried on three dresses, before feeling something click. The sales associate thought so, too. The woman gave Nic a nod and said "that's the one" when she saw her in the sleeveless black sheath with a halter neck. She tried to foist a gaudy rhinestone necklace on her, but Nic politely refused her. She had never been one for much jewelry. She'd worn her class ring until she gave it to Adam, and then she'd worn his on a chain around her neck. Nothing since then. She hadn't seen her class ring in years, though Adam's was still in the top dresser drawer in her room back at home.

At least she thought it was. She didn't go home often, and she certainly hadn't looked for Adam's ring any of those times.

Excited about the office party, and excited about going to Scott's parents' house Christmas night for snacks and games—even though the thought of meeting his family was a little bit terrifying—she was in a silly, happy mood at work Friday. She wasn't a grouchy person, never stiff or uptight, but still, she knew she was smiling more than usual, and she was chattier than usual, and if anyone stopped to consider her behavior and her attitude, they might associate the change with a change in her relationship status; in other words, she knew it was possible her coworkers were speculating that Nic was feeling the holiday spirit because she was gettin' some.

Rather than embarrass her or make her mad, it amused her. Besides, there was a lot more to it than that, a lot more to her and Scott than that. On the other hand, it was kind of true. She hummed a Christmas song—she'd been humming all day, but the song seemed to change by the minute—as she headed to the break room. After seeing everyone munching on Christmas goodies all day, she'd finally decided she was ready for a sugar cookie or a piece of fudge. She heard Jackson 5 singing "I Saw Mommy Kissing Santa Claus" as she walked down the hall, and as had been the case all day, she was instantly humming that one.

Someone had hung mistletoe in the break room sometime this week. There had been a lot of jokes about it, mostly about sexual harassment in the workplace. As far as Nic knew, there hadn't been any heavy lip lock action going on. Not even a European cheek bus. But then, as far as she knew, she and Scott were the only two in the building into each other. She'd seen a few handshakes and bro hugs in the general vicinity of the mistletoe, but everyone was behaving and calling snarky greetings and verbal kisses to each other.

Nic wondered about who would have put the mistletoe there in the first place, especially in the current social culture. But she figured if everyone was behaving, why not? Either way, it wasn't her problem.

She rounded the corner and decided as she entered the break room that she wanted fudge. But when she realized someone was standing under the mistletoe, she stopped in her tracks and stared. His back was to her, but Nic was intimately acquainted with Scott Woodrow's body, and she knew it was Scott with his hands on Hailey's hips and his chest on her boobs. Okay, maybe it was Hailey leaning into him, but there wasn't any breathing room between them. They weren't sharing a passionate kiss, but what Nic watched was almost worse. They were laughing softly, lips close together, talking in soft, intimate voices. The kind she and Scott used when they woke up together after a night of making love.

The thought of trying to swallow anything now—fudge, cheating, a knife—almost made her cough out loud. It would get stuck in her throat. The sight of Scott teasing with Hailey the way they teased and played was stuck in her throat. She eased backwards, unwilling to confront either of them now—her heart was in her throat, too, not to mention they were at work. Hailey noticed her over Scott's shoulder. Nic watched the realization that they'd been caught steal over her, watched her open her mouth —probably to spew a lie or excuses—but Nic shook her head and turned on a heel to walk out. Her eyes burned, so she ducked into the ladies' room for a moment. Hailey could and would find her in here, so she didn't allow herself to fall apart. She didn't give herself a minute in front of the mirror to wonder why Scott would play her if he was interested in Hailey. She didn't think about Callie. She didn't wonder what was wrong with her that she couldn't keep a guy interested. She washed her hands and splashed a bit of cold water on her face and then nearly ran into Hailey as she yanked the door open to go back out and get to work.

"Nic—"

"I'm busy, Hailey," Nic answered quietly.

"You're not, though." Hailey followed her down the empty hall to her cubicle. "Can we talk?"

Nic glanced at her but said nothing.

"You're getting ready to leave." Hailey tossed her hands up. "I know your routine. You're going home."

Nic bit her tongue. She might have a work routine. It might be quitting time for the day, but that didn't mean she was going home. Hailey—no one—knew her routine. Well. Scott did. But she didn't want to think about Scott.

"I really don't want to talk, Hailey," she said on a long, tired sigh. She set her iPad on the corner of her desk and leaned over to get her purse from the drawer.

"Nic, c'mon." Hailey stepped up closer to the desk and touched the back of Nic's elbow. "Please? It's not what you think. You know that."

"What if I think it's just the magic of the season? You guys just got carried away under the mistletoe, right?"

"Yes," Hailey agreed. But when Nic turned to look at her, she shook her head. "No. Not even that, Nic."

"Look." Nic sighed again as she dropped her purse on the edge of the desk. She caught it before it could fall and then rolled her head on her neck. "I'm tired. I'm going home. I'll see you Monday."

"What about the party? Scott said you were going to the party with him."

Nic snorted, but she covered her mouth with her hand and nodded. "Right. Where is Scott, anyway? Why isn't he the one in here groveling?"

"I'm not groveling," Hailey argued. "I'm telling you Scott and I bumped into each other under the mistletoe, and I kissed him on the cheek."

"Right." Nic nodded. "Goodnight, Hailey. See you Monday."

She could take the dress back. Thankfully, she hadn't taken the tags off yet. She hadn't bought new shoes; she'd found a pair of sexy black heels in her closet. She couldn't remember the last time she'd worn them, but she did have to dust them off. Good as new. No matter, she wouldn't feel guilty tossing them to the back of her closet again. She would order pizza or better yet, throw something together at home, and curl up to watch TV. Anything but a Christmas movie. Even an informercial about a carpet shampooer sounded better.

She fished around in her purse for her keys and then pulled the straps up over her shoulder.

"Okay, well, I guess my friendship means nothing to you," Hailey said quietly. Nic stopped dead in her tracks and glanced at Hailey over her shoulder.

"Are you kidding me, Hailey?"

"Well, if that's how much you trust me, I can't change your mind," Hailey mumbled. "But I thought you and Scott were close. He was talking about you. Telling me what he wanted to get you for Christmas. If you don't trust me, I thought you would at least trust him."

Nic blinked and stared after Hailey when she walked away. Funny that Nic had found Hailey and Scott in a compromising situation, but she was the one feeling weird—almost guilty—as she left the station. The drive home was punctuated with fits of frustration and little pinpricks of pain. Her eyes burned, but she didn't cry easily, and there was a tiny little voice inside her head whispering to her that it wasn't what it looked like.

Scott wasn't a player, and it wasn't his promise of such that made Nic believe. Their relationship was new, yes, but she'd known him long enough to know he wasn't that kind of guy. Still, she couldn't ignore the jab of hurt she'd felt when she saw him and Hailey cozied together, teasing, near-kissing, under the mistletoe.

She would take the weekend to think about it. No matter what had been happening in the breakroom, she and Scott had moved pretty fast these past few weeks. Maybe not at the pace of love at first sight—or even lust at first sight—they'd spent some time together before giving into their attraction and sliding into a very intimate relationship. But still, for someone like Nic, someone who didn't trust easily and wasn't inclined to believe in true love, and most definitely not one true love for herself, they had fallen into a pretty serious relationship pretty quickly.

A few days without Scott hovering at her every turn might help clear her head. Her heart. Maybe she was reading their relationship wrong. Maybe this thing with Scott was meant to be a fun, lighthearted hookup to bring her back to the spirit of Christmas. Didn't seem like the kind of thing a higher power would do to wake her up—having her jump in bed with a hot coworker just so she could be reminded that the peace of Christmas was something special. Didn't seem like the stuff of a cheesy Christmas romance novel or movie, either—hooking up for some fun nights to remember how to enjoy the holidays. What then? Would the script have her and Scott ending things by Valentine's Day?

Well, no, the script—if they were following one—had thrown Hailey at her.

Nic pulled into her driveway, relieved to be home. Her head pounded, a sharp throb between her eyes. Maybe she needed some sleep. No doubt she and Scott had burned the midnight oil last weekend. Maybe he didn't sleep much, but she did, and she had certainly lost sleep for him. Not that she would let that happen again. Not now. She was definitely not going to go to bed later and stew over Scott and Hailey kissing under the mistletoe.

She wondered as she unlocked her door and stepped inside if she would feel this way if she had seen a real kiss. If Scott and Hailey had been in a real kiss—mouth to mouth—would she feel that same rush of hurt? Because people kissed under mistletoe. Nic got that. But people who weren't intimately involved didn't kiss and laugh and tease and do those small, sweet kisses under mistletoe. People who weren't involved didn't get cozy and rest their boobs on guys as they kissed playfully under mistletoe.

She had barely closed her door when someone banged on it. Knowing it was Scott, Nic took a deep breath. She dreaded a confrontation, but on the other hand, wouldn't it be better to just get this over with? Otherwise, she would be worrying about it all evening. Not just picturing that scene in her head over and over but worrying about having to talk to Scott about what happened or didn't happen.

"Can I come in?" he asked when she pulled the door open.

Their eyes met, and she was reminded again that Scott wasn't the kind of guy to cheat on a woman. Nor was he the kind of guy to claim kisses with other women and plead his case that it was okay because of the mistletoe. No doubt Nic had read the situation wrong.

But knowing that didn't make her feel any better.

She decided she would rather have seen him kiss Hailey. Anyone could play with physical intimacy, but she'd let Scott in. She'd shared herself with him, and Nic didn't share much of herself with anyone. That's what hurt, she decided. She'd broken her own rules and let Scott in. She'd enjoyed the crazy holiday rush with him. She'd let him bring back that childish wonder of Christmas, and now she felt betrayed, because she'd seen him in that sweet embrace with another woman. No question she was jealous, but it didn't necessarily mean Scott had done anything wrong.

With a sigh and a shrug, she walked away from the door. Scott stepped inside as Nic kicked her shoes off and shrugged out of her coat. Rather than hang it up, she tossed it over the back of a chair, took a second to steel herself to whatever he was going to say, and turned to look at him.

"You know I wasn't in the break room making out with Hailey."

She did, yes, but she wasn't ready to let it go just yet. After all, he was a grown man, and he had allowed himself to get caught there under the mistletoe with a woman who wasn't Nic. She moved without comment, but Scott followed her through the living area to the kitchen.

"Nic."

"Look, Scott, I'm tired. I don't—"

"I had to finish up a few things at work. But I got outta there as soon as I could to come over here."

"Okay." She turned to him and offered him a deep shrug. "Fine."

"Fine?" He tipped his head. "Fine, like, we're fine, and I'm overreacting, and we're going to the party tonight and you're sleeping in my arms tonight? Or fine like you're pissed, and you don't want to talk to me?"

"I'm not pissed," she mumbled. "But I'm not going to the party. And I'll see you Monday."

"What?" He frowned. "What does that even mean?"

"I told you I'm tired. And I'm upset—"

"So, you're upset, but you're not pissed off at me? Nic?" His voice rose an octave as he finished speaking. "I went to grab a piece of fudge, and Hailey was looking at her phone. She reached for a cookie, and we ran into each other."

"Okay." She shrugged again.

"That's it. There was no big kiss."

"Just some little kisses," she said softly.

"Hailey said it's bad luck to not kiss when you're under the mistletoe. And I laughed and told her I was on a run of the best luck of my life, so I didn't want to risk losing that. And the best luck of my life is you, Nic."

Nic huffed out a frustrated sigh and lowered her gaze to the floor. She ignored the nagging feeling, that tiny little déjà vu thing that made her stomach hurt.

"Okay, Scott. I get it. You bumped into each other accidentally, and you laughed about it, and she kissed you so as not to break your streak of good luck."

"Yes, that's what happened. Why are we not going to the party if you're not angry?'

"I just need some time."

Scott lifted his hands and combed his fingers through his hair, clearly frustrated with her.

"You would need time if you believed I was doing something bad. If you thought Hailey and I had a thing going on behind your back."

"I don't believe that, Scott," Nic snapped. "No, I don't believe that. But on the other hand, I just walked in on you with her, and you know how I feel about her, and it wasn't like you were sharing some scorching hot kiss with her. It was worse."

"Worse?" he yelped. "How was it worse? What did I do?"

"You looked happy."

"I was. I was talking about you. She's the one who suggested I come over here to help you with your lights. I thanked her for that. I told her what I'm getting you for Christmas."

Nic shook her head. "No. That's not what I mean. You know what it feels like when we wake up together? And we stay in bed for a few minutes. Just lying together and talking and kissing?"

"Yes."

"That's what it looked like."

"I've never been interested—"

"But that's what it looked like, and I need time to get that out of my head."

"So, that's it? We had a fun few weeks? Like we had some pre-Christmas affair? And now that Christmas is a week away, it's over? Because you saw me talking to Hailey."

"Why Hailey?"

"What do you have against Hailey? What am I missing?"

Nic stood still and drew in a deep breath. "Goodnight, Scott. I'll see you Monday."

"I'm not leaving."

"I'm done—"

"I'm not leaving until you explain this to me. What's the deal with Hailey? Nic, I—"

"Hailey reminds me of Callie," she answered quietly. "Every time I look at her, I see my little sister."

Scott sighed and hung his head. Nic watched him squeeze the back of his neck and shuffle his feet.

"You've never told me the story about you and Callie," he mumbled.

"No, I haven't." She shook her head when he flicked his gaze up to look at her.

"And you won't."

"Not right now, no." She folded her arms over her chest. "How would you feel if you had walked in on me with Joe? Or Kent?"

"I'd be pissed," he answered immediately, "but I would listen to you, and if you insisted it was nothing, I would believe you."

"I do believe you, Scott," she assured him. "But that doesn't make me feel like going to a Christmas party. I'm not in the mood for people now, especially people at work."

"No one else even knows what happened."

Nic shrugged and shook her head. "I'm not up for the noise. Sure not up for putting on a dress and heels and pretending to be something I'm not."

"And what is that, Nic? What would you be pretending to be?"

"Sexy, Scott. There's nothing less sexy than a woman playing dress up and trying to be impressive."

"Nic."

"I'll talk to you Monday."

"I'll stay here."

"No," she answered sharply. "You go."

"Nic, I'm in love with you."

"Funny time for you to say those words," she whispered. "Goodnight, Scott."

She left him in the kitchen and padded down the hall to her bedroom, where she closed the door and leaned back on it, eyes on her bed. Tears burned her eyes again. She remembered the first time they were together, when he had made love to her. The tenderness in his touch and his kisses. She thought of the times she had seen Scott and Hailey together at work, minus the damned mistletoe.

He'd left the mistletoe on her dresser that first night she'd invited him into her bedroom. They had joked about hanging it over the bed, and then much later, after they had become intimately acquainted with each other's bodies, they'd joked more about other places to put it. Now, Nic reached out and touched it, the plain sprig of greenery that claimed kisses and luck. It wasn't pretty like holly and ivy, but it was certainly a Christmas tradition for some people.

She wasn't angry with Scott. She was hurt, but even so, she knew Scott wouldn't treat her or Hailey that way. Nope. Nic's issue tonight was the same issue she'd been carrying for over ten years. She didn't trust anyone completely, not after the way things had ended with Adam. Not after Callie's senior prom.

Deciding she had to tell Scott, that she had to apologize to him, she opened her door and hurried out to the kitchen. When she didn't find him, she rushed to the living room, but he was gone.

TWENTY

Scott yanked at his tie and then slipped two fingers behind the collar of his shirt and tried to stretch it a bit. The damned thing was too tight, and it was uncomfortably hot in the cocktail bar at the country club. He shouldn't have come. He supposed he understood that Nic was upset; even if she believed him about the mistletoe incident—and he wasn't entirely sure that she did—seeing him with Hailey had hurt her. He would feel the same in her shoes. But he would have insisted they talk about it, about everything that might have anything to do with what they were feeling, like Hailey and how she reminded Nic of Callie.

He figured Callie had done something to betray Nic at some point in their pasts, but it was unfair of Nic to take that out on him. When he left Nic's house earlier, he had considered staying home to nurse his anger. But he wasn't that kind of guy. If anything, he needed to be around people to put that frustration on the back burner and let

Nic work through her feelings and decide if she wanted to pursue what they had started.

As soon as the party got started, Hailey and Wyatt had announced the Christmas lights contest winner, obviously not Nic. The Kroeger family; Scott doubted they would be donating the money back to the schools. Not that he blamed them, but he was wallowing over being at the party alone, so he figured he would include them in his bad mood, too.

Now that he was here, listening to his coworkers who happened to be friends, he desperately wanted to go home. In the bar, there were a few small groups of people sipping mixed drinks and talking. Out in the main part of the club— decorated like a winter wonderland—couples were dancing. Scott had looked forward to dancing with Nic. Now that that idea was shot to hell, he was miserable and ready to go.

Dinner had been delicious, but he had picked at his prime rib and sipped his beer so slowly, it was warm before he finished the bottle. He had talked to Hailey, and though there was nothing to feel guilty about, he kept a good distance between them at all times. He sure didn't dance with anyone else, but he didn't want to, anyway.

He stood at the bar now and drained his second beer, another he nursed into room temperature. It was almost nine; surely, he had been here long enough to be socially acceptable, and he was free to go home and wallow alone. He hadn't told anyone at the party what had happened. When asked where Nic was, Scott had simply said she wasn't feeling up to a party and left it at that.

After a quick, quiet goodbye to his friends in the bar, Scott slipped out to the main room to find Hailey and say goodnight. Their eyes connected across the floor; Scott nodded to the door and mouthed the word *goodnight*. Hailey stared back, wide-eyed, and shook her head enthusiastically.

Rather than get dragged into a long conversation, Scott purposely misread her signal that she didn't want him to leave. He tossed her a wave and turned away, even as she squeezed between dancing couples to catch him.

"Scott, wait." She caught up to him near the doors. Scott, fully aware of the mistletoe hanging there, ducked to the side as Hailey slipped her fingers in his.

"This isn't fun without Nic, Hailey," he told her before she could argue any reasons why he should stay. "I'm going home."

"You can't go," Hailey insisted. "Nic's here."

"What?" he snapped. He turned to look, eyes roaming over the dancing crowd. The room was done up with flocked Christmas trees, decorated in crème and silver bells and ribbons. Guys in suits and women in fancy dresses of black and green and red from all the departments at the station shuffled now to some upbeat pop song, but Scott didn't see Nic.

"She's here," Hailey said again. "She came in about five minutes ago."

"Hailey." Scott sighed.

"I'm not kidding. She just went toward the bar. You just missed her."

He narrowed his eyes at her and looked back at the dancing crowd as the music changed to something slow and sexy.

"Seriously?" he asked Hailey.

"I was standing over there with Joe, and I saw her walk in. She looks incredible, Scott. You have to find her."

"What if she doesn't want to see me?" He winced at how surly he sounded, but he was disappointed in how the evening had turned out. He'd toyed with the idea of giving Nic her gift tonight after the party. The delicate white gold necklace with the tiny tree pendant would be perfect for his woman; he had noticed she wasn't into jewelry, but he thought she would appreciate something simple, something with a special meaning.

Now he wasn't sure about anything.

"She's looking for you, Scott." Hailey rolled her eyes. "I know that look on a woman's face."

Scott sucked in a long, deep breath, nodded at Hailey, and went back through the throng of people to the cocktail bar. The music playing now was a slow, jazzy number that sounded like Norah Jones. It was a little bit sexy, and it made that meanness inside him want to rear its head and growl.

He wanted Nic in his arms.

The scene in the bar was the same as it had been minutes earlier when he had walked out. If Hailey had seen Nic head this way, she had already moved on. Scott wasn't sure Hailey had seen her; maybe it was wishful thinking. No matter what Nic had against Hailey, it didn't seem to be mutual.

He turned around, ready to take one more glance at the dancing couples, and then head for home. Nic stood in front of him, only she was dressed in a sexy black dress and spiked heels that gave him all sorts of sexy, x-rated thoughts.

"Scott." Her lips—painted a soft, frosted pink—spoke

his name so softly, for a moment, he wondered if he had imagined it. He might wonder if he was hallucinating—that wishful thinking thing again—except that Nic lifted her hand to touch him. Scott tipped his chin down to see her fingers pressed to his chest. Her fingernails were finished with a clear polish; her fingers and arms bare to her shoulders. Scott dragged his eyes over her shapely arms and imagined them wound around his neck, her smooth, soft thighs wrapped around his hips, and those heels locked behind his butt.

Mouth dry, he couldn't swallow, and instead, he coughed a bit and wished for a drink. Something a bit stronger than the beer he'd just finished. Nic was a vision in the black dress with her hair styled in big, loose curls. She had played up her blue eyes with black eyeliner and a pale lavender shadow; Scott loved her everyday look, but she was stunning right now, staring up at him.

"Nic."

"Can we talk?"

He swallowed hard, but his mouth and throat were still dry. With a nod, he moved closer to her and slipped his arms around her.

"You look beautiful." He pulled her close and rested his chin on her head. "You're here."

Nic lifted her hands to rest them on his shoulders. Scott smoothed his hand down over her hip, careful to behave here in front of the entire workforce of the station. His fingers itched to move further south and clutch her to yank her middle firmly against his erection to stake his claim.

"I tried to catch you before you left," she whispered, face turned to his neck.

"Why didn't you call me?"

They swayed just slightly to the music, both of them oblivious to everyone around them.

"When I realized you were gone, I was afraid I pushed too hard. That you would decide I wasn't worth the trouble."

"I told you I'm in love with you, Nic," he reminded her. "You know there's nothing between me and Hailey."

She nodded, the movement causing her hair to brush over his chin. Scott was already used to waking up to the tickle of her hair on his chin and his chest. He closed his eyes now, relieved to be holding her again.

"I'm sorry," she whispered.

Even though what Nic had seen earlier was innocent, it was ridiculous to think it wouldn't hurt her. She might have reacted wrongly to something simple, but Scott didn't believe she owed him an apology.

When the song ended, Scott kissed her cheek.

"Can we talk?" She slid her hands down from his shoulders but clutched his upper arms.

"Of course."

He ushered her away from the bar, his hand on her lower back as they moved carefully past the dancing crowd to the patio doors. Scott hesitated, though, and touched her arm when she pushed the door open.

"You'll be cold," he argued.

"It's not that bad outside." She stepped through the door. Scott followed her, slipping his sport coat off as he did. When he settled it over her shoulders and she offered him that small, cautious smile, his heart soared. "I should have grabbed a glass of wine."

His heart faltered a bit. He arched his eyebrows at her in askance.

"Is this going to be one of those conversations?"

Her soft, sad laugh made his chest ache.

"No." She hunched her shoulders and huddled deeper into his coat. "I hope not."

"Do you want me to get you a drink?"

"No. Thank you, but no." She sounded breathless. "I owe you an explanation—"

"You don't owe me one," he said quietly, "but I would like to know what's on your mind."

"When I was nineteen, my boyfriend and I had been together for two years. We had that high school sweetheart kind of love going. Like if things had been different, I might have married him and had his children and moved somewhere far away."

Scott bit his lip to keep his mouth shut. He hated that something had hurt her, but this was the journey that had led her to him. He was grateful things had worked out this way.

"He hadn't proposed, but we talked about the future in that general way. We knew we wanted to be together."

"What happened?" His gruff voice caught her attention, and Nic met his eyes.

"My sister didn't have a date for prom," she continued. "Which I find suspicious, because Callie's gorgeous. She was popular. She was nice enough, and up until then, we got along okay most of the time."

"I can't imagine Callie being any more gorgeous than you are."

Nic frowned, but she didn't say anything.

"My mom had this brilliant idea that Adam should take Callie to prom."

"She what?"

"Why wouldn't Callie's big sister want her to go to prom? Adam could take her. It wouldn't hurt me to do some reading for school, and Adam and Callie could go to prom."

"That's ridiculous."

Nic shrugged and looked away, but she tipped her head up to acknowledge his comment.

"I told you Mom babies her," she said quietly. "She wasn't sick. She wasn't particularly weak. She was premature, and she was small for her age, but there was nothing wrong with Callie. Even our pediatrician told Mom that all the time. But still. Mom favored Callie. Wanted her to have everything she wanted."

"And she wanted a prom date."

"Maybe." Nic shrugged. "I've never worked out if Callie wanted a date. Or if Callie wanted Adam."

Scott flinched. "Please don't tell me Adams is her husband."

"No." Nic groaned. "God, no. They went to prom. They went to her friend's after-party. Adam brought her home the next morning. Callie thanked me. Adam and I went out that night. But." She shook her head. "Callie promised me nothing happened. She said he kissed her cheek when he brought her home, but I didn't believe her. It's not that I think she slept with him, but she acted squirrely about it, and so something never felt right about it."

"What happened with you and Adam?"

Nic shrugged. "We grew apart. He was out of town for

school, so we didn't see each other often. When he did come home, things were strained between us. I would look at him and wonder how they danced. What they said to each other. If something happened."

"That's horrible."

"I didn't want to be with him. Not with all the doubts. His parents moved away when he was still away at school, so I was the only reason for him to come back. And we decided we needed to go our own way."

"What did Callie say?"

"She never said much," Nic answered. "But we grew apart, too. She won't look me in the eyes now. Never wants to do much with me. She acts—"

"Guilty," Scott finished her sentence.

"Yeah."

"So, was Adam the big love of your life?" Scott fought a shiver and plunged his hands in his hip pockets. He hoped Nic didn't notice he was holding his breath, waiting for her to answer.

"No." She held his gaze steady. "Not at all. I wish him well. It just...the way Callie has acted about it all these years...it hurts more that I lost my sister."

"Do you talk to her at all?"

"Yeah. We're polite. Sort of. She pushes to be involved in my life, but only so far. Like she knows she's not welcome, and she knows why."

"So, what did Hailey do that reminds you of Callie?"

"Nothing," Nic admitted. "But I look at her and see Callie."

Scott couldn't hide his surprise at her answer.

"I know. It's not fair of me to hold a grudge against Hailey because she looks like my sister. To be fair, I don't trust a lot of people. I mean, it's not like Callie wrecked my marriage. It's not like I lost a life to her, but I just...I wonder sometimes if my mom and Cal were in it together. I know that sounds ridiculous when I say it out loud."

"It doesn't."

"I just...I like my life the way it is. The way it's been for the past several years. I don't let a lot of people in, Scott. I never let Pete get this close."

"You lived with Pete," he reminded her.

"I did," she agreed with a nod, "but I didn't love him."

"You love me?"

There were those wings on his heart again. Scott held his breath and rocked up on the toes of his feet. He was cold; Nic had to be freezing, but damned if he was going to cut this conversation short just to go inside and warm up.

"I do love you," she whispered, "and finding you under the mistletoe with Hailey just caught me off guard and I reacted badly. I'm still carrying around bad feelings for Callie, and it's Callie I need to confront about that. Not you."

Scott whooshed out the breath he had been holding.

"C'mere." He pulled his hands from his pockets to reach for her. Nic moved closer to him and pressed her head to his chin.

"I'm sorry," she said again.

"You love me?" he said again, hands flat on her back.

"I love you, Scott." She turned her face to his and kissed the corner of his mouth.

His heart climbed again, and his stomach flip-flopped. He captured her lips to kiss her again, suddenly warm enough to be out here with her the rest of the night.

"There's mistletoe in the vestibule," he said when he ended the kiss.

"I told you you've never needed mistletoe to kiss me."

"Might be warmer inside." He held her close.

"It is a little cold out here."

"The dress is very sexy."

Nic wiggled against him.

"I would love to go back inside and dance with the most beautiful woman in the room."

"Funny." She offered him the feisty grin that drove him wild. "I'd really like to dance with you."

"I wanna be with you tonight, Nic."

She drew back just far enough to look him in the eyes.

"Still have the mistletoe in my bedroom."

TWENTY-ONE

Nic sipped her coffee absently as she watched her nieces playing the new dance game from her mother. What a perfect Christmas. She and Scott had spent every night together since the office party. Thankfully, she had come to her senses and gone after him that night. It would have been even harder to accept if she had lost him because she'd pushed him away over something that she needed to change within herself and her relationship with her sister.

Christmas Eve had been the best she'd had since she was a kid at home with her parents and Callie. She and Scott had cooked together; Scott pulled together a fancy pork loin, and Nic had prepared a fancy carrot side dish to add to their baked potatoes. Later, after dinner, they snuggled close on the sofa to watch Christmas movies until Nic needed toothpicks to keep her eyelids pried open.

Of course, once they were in her bed, she was magically awake, and they had made love before they curled together to sleep. Likewise, Christmas morning, they lingered in her bed, sharing Christmas kisses and more before finally getting up and showering and dressing for Nic's mom's house. She had been apprehensive about introducing Scott to her mother, but maybe because he knew the history between Nic and her mom and sister, it went well. She hadn't realized how worried she was about it until after the fact when she joined her mom in the kitchen to help serve the brunch she had prepared. Scott sat comfortably with Nic's dad and the few other guests there and talked as if he had always been part of the family.

Then again, that was the first thing that had drawn Nic to him. Scott was kind-hearted and fun to talk to; her parents certainly seemed to agree. She didn't need to worry that her mom would try to steal Scott away from her and give him to Callie, but she did still want to guard him from anything of the sort. Twice her mother had mentioned Callie—that she was an incredible cook and that she was a fitness nut—but each time, Scott had steered the conversation back to Nic and told her mother that Nic was also an incredible cook and that they were exploring fitness options together. Nic had snickered at that last comment, because so far, the only fitness they were doing was extreme couples' fitness. Nic loved sex with Scott, and he had proven himself very fit and capable of getting down and dirty for a little fun, but she didn't particularly want to share that tidbit with her mom or sister.

Nic had felt the same sort of ease with Scott's family later that same evening. She looked forward to getting to know his sisters better, and she loved being around the kids.

"What're you grinning about?" Callie asked her now.

"Hmm?" Nic stirred from her thoughts and glanced at her sister.

"The grin on your face does not match the level of excitement an aunt should feel watching her nieces dance to a video game's instructions."

Nic laughed softly. "Thinking about Scott."

"You love him."

"I do." Nic nodded. "I...almost pushed him away. And then I realized the issue I thought was ours, his and mine, is more my issue."

"You don't trust easily, Nic." Callie sighed. "And I know it's my fault."

Nic eyed Callie silently.

"You did everything for me," Callie continued. "When we were kids. You were the best big sister ever. And the one thing you didn't want to give me, I took from you anyway."

"Why?" Nic whispered. "Why did you do it?"

"Do you still love Adam?"

"No," Nic answered with a deep shrug. "I don't. But I did then, and it hurt the way it all played out."

Callie pursed her lips and nodded. "I know. I'm sorry."

"Did you sleep with him?"

"No." Callie met Nic's eyes and held her gaze. "I didn't. It all happened just like I said it did. Adam was fun. He treated me like a friend. Like a kid sister. He kissed me goodbye when he brought me home. Just a kiss on my cheek. Nothing happened. I don't think I wanted anything to happen."

"You just wanted—what? To know you could do it? Take my boyfriend if you wanted to?"

"It wasn't that I wanted your boyfriend," Callie argued. She took a deep breath and closed her eyes. "I just...you always gave me everything, and I was just selfish? Greedy, I guess. So, I thought I would get Adam to take me to prom. I think I wanted to see how far I could push you before you said no."

"Nice." Nic bit her lip. "You always acted so guilty about it. I thought you slept with him."

"I felt guilty for lying to Mom. Telling her I didn't have a date. Three guys in my class asked me to prom. I told them all no. And then poured it on for Mom that I didn't have a date."

"Wow, Callie." Nic rubbed her eyes and then pinched the bridge of her nose.

"I know. I'm sorry, Nic. I really am." Callie spoke sincerely. "It wasn't worth it. I had fun with Adam, but I lost you. I might have cost you a lifetime with someone you loved. I think about that a lot."

"Adam and I wouldn't have stayed together, Cal," Nic mumbled. "We were just kids. But I was so sure you slept with him that I never wanted to be in love again, and I sure never planned to introduce you to someone I might love again."

"I'm happy now," Callie told her. "With my life. But Nic, even if I weren't? If I weren't married? Didn't have the girls? I would never do that again. I took advantage of you. You deserve to be happy with Scott."

Nic couldn't help the big grin that tipped her lips up. She ducked her head and shrugged.

"He's pretty great," she said wistfully. "I wanted to

murder him and Hailey when he showed up to help me with the lights, but it worked out."

"Too bad you didn't win." Callie nudged Nic's leg with her foot.

"I didn't win the lights contest, but I got Scott." Nic shrugged. "I won bigger."

Nic turned and watched as Scott joined her nieces in front of her parents' big screen TV. She and Callie laughed as he tried to keep up with the dance steps on the game.

"Hey." Scott turned and pointed at her. "You. You're next."

GETTIN' HITCHED

Chapter 1

Mercedes Ingalls slowed her car to a stop and leaned forward to squint through the windshield at the big brick home to her right. An ornate wooden front door, flanked on both sides by ornate sidelights, gave the two-story brick house a snooty, aristocratic appearance. But the bike thrown down in the front yard and the soccer goal tipped over near the drive were clearly the mark of kids, and though Mercedes thought Nicholas Moore's kids were too young to ride bikes that size, she pulled her little Corolla over to the curb to park.

She consulted her phone again, where she'd typed the Moore address into her notes app. 4769 Stardust. Her maxi skirt felt all wrong now. If the Moore kids were old enough to ride a bike that size, somehow wearing a maxi skirt to the interview felt wrong. Maybe she should have worn khakis.

"Too late to worry about it now, Cedes," she mumbled as she swung her car door shut. The mailboxes out here were the fancy kind covered in bricks made to look like miniature houses. No numbers visible anywhere, so she couldn't be sure this was 4769. A beat-up pickup truck was parked across the street, and the garage door at that house was open. But there was no one in sight to ask if she was at Nicholas Moore's house, so she would just have to ring the doorbell and find out.

Mercedes eyed the pristine lawn as she made her way up the driveway. The bike and the soccer goal felt terribly out of place with the perfectly trimmed edges of grass and the vividly colored flowers in what appeared to be professionally done landscaping. An electronic beat pounded faintly from deep inside the house as Mercedes stepped up on the porch and lifted her hand to press the doorbell with her thumb.

She drew her hand away from the doorbell and studied the chipped robin's egg blue polish on her thumbnail. If she got this job, she could maybe start doing professional manicures again. Or at least, maybe she could afford a new bottle of nail polish. What she had now was old and chunky.

When no one answered the door—probably hadn't heard the bell with that music blaring inside—she looked over her shoulder and spotted a guy across the street. He appeared to be heading to the truck at the curb. Mercedes shifted her weight on her feet and turned to get a better look at him. Her movement must have caught his eye, because he waved and hollered hello. Deciding she might have better luck asking him about where Nicholas Moore lived, she stepped off the porch and headed back down the drive.

"Hey."

"Hi." She flashed him a smile as she crossed the street. "Any chance you can tell me which house is Nicholas Moore's?"

"This is Nick's house." The guy met her in the middle of the drive. Mercedes eyed the way his longish, brown hair curled at his crew cut shirt collar and the shock of the same curls that fell over his eyebrow. Broad shoulders filled out the faded brown T-shirt—Mercedes thought the letters across the front spelled race, but the letters, too, were faded, and given that the body under the letters appeared to be textbook perfection, she didn't want to stare too hard. Loose board shorts hung on his hips, though he was anything but scrawny. His long lean legs had been kissed by the sun—

Mercedes gave herself a mental shake. She'd been reading too many romance novels. Time to switch gears and read a thriller or a spy novel. Anything but something that talked about sun-kissed skin and finely chiseled lips and the perfect amount of scruff—

"Doorbell doesn't work," the guy told her as he offered her both a friendly smile and a handshake. "Are you here about the babysitting thing?"

"Nanny," she mumbled, wondering if this guy was actually Nick Moore. Could she be that lucky? She nodded when she realized she had barely mumbled the word and the guy was watching her curiously. Not only was his body textbook perfection, so was his face. Classic bone structure, a perfect arch in his thick eyebrows, and eyes the color of the ocean as the sun sank in the west and darkness merged with the lighter blue waters.

"I'm Parker," he told her. "Nick's brother."

Of course, this couldn't be Nicholas.

Mercedes caught herself before a disappointed sigh could slip out. It didn't matter what Nicholas looked like; she was here to score a nanny position, not a date with the dad. Who was probably married, although nowhere in the five-line job description and contact information did it say anything other than Nicholas Moore.

No matter, Mercedes reminded herself. She wasn't interested in finding a date. She wanted a job. Specifically, a job that would give her some nights and weekends off.

"Mercedes."

The guy had a firm grip, and if anything, his smile grew bigger and more inviting, but there was no telltale romance-novel zing. She didn't have a sudden urge to hold tight to his hand or to snuggle up close to him and press her face to his.

"Nick's inside. In the office."

"Okay." She nodded as the guy dropped her hand and backed away slowly. The worn flip-flops that completed his outfit screamed surfer dude, but being that they were standing in midwestern Illinois and nowhere near a coast, she doubted he had a surfboard stashed in the truck bed.

As if she would simply know where the office was once inside the house, the guy turned and headed down the drive to his truck. Mercedes watched him for a second, but she shifted her gaze back to the house and wondered what Nicholas would be like.

Should she just go on in? Parker's words and actions kind of insinuated that she should. Behind her, the truck came to life with a pretty, low rumble, bringing to mind exes who drove monster trucks and motorcycles. Mercedes chuckled as she tapped on the front door. Rather than stand here and wait and hope Nicholas heard her—she was already late—she twisted the knob and when she found it unlocked, she pushed it open just a smidge.

She peeked her head into a neat little entry way. Slate gray tiles on the floor in front of the door butted up against the snowy white carpet of the living room. A black baby grand dominated the far side of the room, though a big screen TV hung on the east wall. Two gray wing-backed chairs faced the piano, a white leather loveseat faced the TV.

Mercedes held her breath as she stepped inside. Kids lived here? And the carpet was still white?

"Mr. Moore?" she called now as she pushed the door closed behind her. "Mr. Moore, it's Mercedes. Your brother said the doorbell doesn't work."

She heard a deep male voice rambling about tech-nology—something about design and protocol, not that she cared. The voice grew louder to her right. She looked up just as another beautiful man appeared at the end of a hallway on the east side of the house. There was a resem-blance between this guy and the brother who had just left. Nicholas Moore had the same eye color; though his hair was a bit lighter, definitely shorter. A little long for busi-ness casual, but Mercedes liked the way it curled over the collar of his dress shirt.

When their eyes met, she started to say something, but he gave her a slight shake of his head. He lifted his finger to stop her and spoke again, this time talking about numbers and projections. He turned his head just enough that Mercedes saw he had a Bluetooth earpiece in his right ear. She closed her mouth, prepared to wait him out.

She let her gaze roam to a small formal dining room to

her left. The ornate white marble table could seat six. The upright iron chairs covered in dove grey cushions looked pretentious and uncomfortable. Abstract art in shades of grays and golds hung on the southern wall. The longer Mercedes stared at the twisted lines and splashes of color, the more her head hurt. Instead, she turned to look her fill at Nicholas Moore while he was otherwise occupied.

He wore charcoal gray trousers—they were expensive, Mercedes could tell from looking—and a lavender dress shirt. The collar was unbuttoned; his sleeves were rolled up to reveal his forearms. A fancy gold watch decorated his left wrist, but his fingers were bare.

Which, Mercedes reminded herself, didn't mean anything. Some men didn't wear wedding rings.

Not that it mattered one way or another to her.

She noticed he was wearing wingtips and wondered if he always appeared this uptight or if it was simply the hassle of hiring a new nanny. Or…a nanny. Did they have to let someone go? Or maybe their nanny quit or moved away?

"Mercedes?"

She wondered where the kids were now. It was awfully quiet in here for children of any age, and though the description hadn't specifically said *how many* children of *what age*, Mercedes thought there should be some kind of noise.

Poor kids.

She couldn't imagine living in a beautiful, cold house like this when she was younger. She and her brother had been holy terrors when they were kids; thankfully, her parents had given them a lot of freedom to grow up and learn on their own. Some people thought she and Aaron had too much freedom. Mercedes thought some people had too much time on their hands if they needed to worry so much about how she and Aaron were raised.

"Ms. Ingalls?"

She snapped to attention at the use of her last name. Nicholas Moore pulled the Bluetooth piece from his ear and stared at her expectantly now.

"Yes."

"We can talk in the office."

ABOUT THE AUTHOR

Tracy is the author of the Lorelei Bluffs women's fiction series, the Williams Legacy, and several stand-alone women's fiction novels. She has recently dabbled in contemporary romance, as well.

For more information about Tracy or her books, visit her online at www.broemmerbooks.com

ALSO BY TRACY BROEMMER

Women's Fiction Novels:

Luther's Cross (Writing as Therese Kinkaide)

Luther's Cross 10th Anniversary Edition (Tracy Broemmer)

Fairytale (Writing as Therese Kinkaide)

Just Like Them (Writing as Therese Kinkaide)

Small Hours (Writing as Therese Kinkaide)

Picket Fences

Two Story Home

Green-Eyed Girl

Say Everything

Come Home For Christmas

Sketching Litchfield Lake

Ever, Again

Safe as Houses

Damsel

Every Little Thing, Lorelei Bluffs, Book 1

Two A.M., Lorelei Bluffs, Book 2

Blind, Lorelei Bluffs, Book 3

Leaving July, Lorelei Bluffs, Book 4

Hesitation Marks, Lorelei Bluffs, Book 5

Four Letter Words, Lorelei Bluffs, Book 6

See Kate, Lorelei Bluffs, Book 7

Loved You More, Lorelei Bluffs, Book 8

A Lorelei Ending, Lorelei Bluffs, Book 9

I Do, Lorelei Bluffs, Book 10

Truth Is, The Williams Legacy, Book 1

Other People's Ugly, The Williams Legacy, Book 2

Omissions, The Williams Legacy, Book 3

Contemporary Romance Novels:

Destiny's Calling: Your Future Is Waiting

Wedding Day Shenanigans

Holiday Fling

The Kiss Off

Something Like Love

Love, Nashville, The Mississippi Queen Trilogy, Book 1

Forever, Duncan, The Mississippi Queen Trilogy, Book 2

Always, Jess, The Mississippi Queen Trilogy, Book 3

Gettin' Hitched, The H Books, Book 1

Contemporary Romance Novellas:

Indian Summer, A Novella

Dear Jaclyn Perris, A Novella

Contemporary Romance Short Stories:

Perfect Pictures, The Wine Tasting Series, Traminette

Coming Home, The Wine Tasting Series, Edelweiss

Save Me Every Dance, The Wine Tasting Series, Rosé

Marry Me, The Wine Tasting Series, Shiraz

Birthday Wishes, The Wine Tasting Series, Muscat

Dad Jeans, The Wine Tasting Series, Vignoles